Hours later, Jace groaned. "That's your phone, not mine. Switch it off," he urged.

Gigi rolled naked out of bed in the daylight filtering through the curtains and dug through the pile of clothes spread across the floor to find her jeans and answer her phone.

"Miss Campbell?" the polite voice began. "This is a confidential call. Could you give me your details before I give you the test result?"

It was the laboratory. As Gigi answered the questions to prove her identity, she paused. Jace had sat up in bed, shrewd eyes as green as polished emeralds pinned to her sudden pallor and the tension etched in her fine-boned features. She pushed the phone back into the pocket of her jeans. "I'm pregnant," she whispered shakily in total shock and denial, perspiration breaking out on her brow.

GREEK'S SHOTGUN WEDDING

LYNNE GRAHAM

PRESENTS

Harlequin® PRESENTS™

Recycling programs for this product may not exist in your area.

ISBN-13: 978-1-335-93930-2

Greek's Shotgun Wedding

Harlequin Enterprises ULC
22 Adelaide St. West, 41st Floor
Toronto, Ontario M5H 4E3, Canada
www.Harlequin.com

Printed in Lithuania

MIX
Paper | Supporting responsible forestry
FSC® C021394

Lynne Graham was born in Northern Ireland and has been a keen romance reader since her teens. She is very happily married to an understanding husband who has learned to cook since she started to write! Her five children keep her on her toes. She has a very large dog who knocks everything over, a very small terrier who barks a lot and two cats. When time allows, Lynne is a keen gardener.

Books by Lynne Graham

Harlequin Presents

The Italian's Bride Worth Billions
The Baby the Desert King Must Claim
Two Secrets to Shock the Italian

The Stefanos Legacy

Promoted to the Greek's Wife
The Heirs His Housekeeper Carried
The King's Christmas Heir

Cinderella Sisters for Billionaires

The Maid Married to the Billionaire
The Maid's Pregnancy Bombshell

The Diamond Club

Baby Worth Billions

Visit the Author Profile page at Harlequin.com for more titles.

CHAPTER ONE

'I THOUGHT YOU were planning to be a no-show,' Jace's uncle Evander told his six-foot-four-inch-tall nephew.

Jace strode away from the helicopter with the silver logo flash that announced that the billionaire owner of Diamandis Industries had finally arrived for the funeral proceedings.

Apologising for his late arrival, Jace dealt the older man a regretful smile in which resentment, respect and fondness were all contained. Evander and his British husband, Marcus, had, after all, raised Jace when his own father refused to do so. Of course, both Jace and his uncle had been the *outsiders* in the Diamandis circle, Evander because he was gay and refused to pretend otherwise and Jace because his father, Argus, had refused to act as a parent and had abandoned his son at the tender age of six.

In actuality, Jace had lost both his parents on the same day. His mother had been an internationally acclaimed and famously glamorous opera singer, who had walked out on Argus for another man that day, leaving her son behind. When she and her lover crashed their car and died a few hours afterwards, Jace's father had burst into gales of hysterical laughter. And then he had looked only once at the little boy staring at him with his late wife's bright green eyes and her mop of curls before tucking Jace and his nanny into a limousine to be taken to his parents' estate, thereby repudiating his firstborn son.

It was a decision that Argus had never revisited over the twenty-two years that had followed…and now he was dead. Jace had indelibly remained a reminder of his father's lowest moment, a moment when not all the money in the world could compensate a man's hurt pride or save his shiny public image from malicious gossip about cuckolds. Even though he quickly remarried and had a second son, Argus had continued to reject Jace as his child. At one stage he had also attempted to cut Jace out of the family inheritance and give it instead to Jace's half-brother, Domenico, only to be prevented by their grandfather's lawyers.

Jace hadn't wanted to play the hypocrite and attend his reluctant father's funeral. Evander, however, had taken a very different stance. Evander had argued vehemently with Jace, pointing out that his nephew might be only twenty-eight years old and single but he was now the *de facto* head of the Diamandis family, and that it was a matter of good taste and common sense to accept his rightful place. Before Jace could think too much about it, he was engulfed in an embrace by his grandmother, Electra Diamandis. And if she could comfortably attend her son's funeral when the two of them had lived at daggers drawn, he believed that he had even less to complain about.

Jace was currently the cynosure of all eyes. 'Why are they all staring at me?' he murmured as they emerged from the church.

'You're worth billions and they don't know you,' his uncle reminded him wryly. 'Bet they are now wincing for all the times they cut you dead.'

'None of them wanted to know me while I was growing up, apart from you and Marcus,' Jace agreed grimly. 'You took in the poisoned chalice and didn't care about keeping Argus sweet.'

'All your little nubile cousins have got wedding rings gleaming in their eyes,' Evander warned him, half under his breath.

Jace laughed with sudden intense amusement. 'I learned my lesson well with Seraphina.'

An unexpected smile curved his uncle's mouth. 'Yes, I did very much enjoy that visit from my brother Adonis when he demanded you marry my niece for stealing her virtue. You see, you can't go tantalising them all with the headlines you make and not expect to become a target for the gold-diggers in the family.'

'I'm all grown up now and rather more staid—'

'Absolute lies,' Marcus interrupted from his other side. 'Ain't nothing staid about your playboy lifestyle.'

'I'm only going to be young once,' Jace countered with raw assurance. Yet he remained grateful to the couple who had raised him with love, loyalty and care.

A more conventional set of parentals might have given up on him when he went through an extended wild period as a teenager. Marcus and Evander, however, had stuck by him through thick and thin and he would never forget the debt he owed them for the security and stability they had given him.

'But you're heading towards thirty and you've never had a relationship with a woman,' Evander quipped. 'Maybe you need to think about that—'

'I don't do relationships.' Hell, no! Jace thought in horror. He did sex, not relationships. He kept his private life simple and straightforward. Since he had attained adulthood, no dates, no serious discussions with women and no boundaries had ever featured in his world. He did as he liked, when he liked and with whom he liked. And in truth, he honestly believed that he was happier embracing his freedom that way.

'You need to try it…at least once,' his uncle said.

Jace gritted his even white teeth. 'How much longer do I need to stay?' he breathed, feeling like a teenager again, but he hated it all *so much:* all the fawning attention from people who had ignored him all his life to meet Argus's expectations and curry his father's favour and *now*? The constant sidewise glances, the supposedly friendly grieving comments. As if he cared an atom for the father he had hardly known, who had hurt him beyond belief as a child when he'd chosen to punish him for his mother's sins!

'Speak to your brother before you leave. You don't

need to do drinks and chat with the rest of them. You don't owe them anything,' his uncle told him.

'Why should *I* speak to Domenico?' Jace queried in a tone of literal disbelief.

'He had nothing to do with any of it and you're the *big* brother,' Evander reminded him drily. 'You've never even met him. Five minutes, Jace. He's the closest relative you have left alive. Make us proud...*please*—'

Jace breathed in slow and deep, rage hurtling through his big powerful frame at that piece of advice. But then he thought it through for the first time in many years and his temper receded because as always there was a lot of logic in Evander's words. Their father was dead now. Maybe there *was* room for him to look again at that particular relationship. It wasn't his brother's fault that Jace had been rejected, ignored and threatened with disinheritance. For all he knew, Argus had been a lousy parent to Domenico as well.

And affecting not to hear the remarks or see the languishing glances cast in his direction, Jace went off to meet his half-brother for the first time...

'What in the world...?' Gigi marvelled out loud as she stood at her front window and glimpsed the large animal dancing through the traffic with a dangling lead still attached to its collar.

Snowy, the ragged cockatoo in the corner cage in the sitting room, tried to mimic her voice—not very well. Humphrey the tortoise ambled in, munching a lettuce leaf. Hoppy, the terrier dozing on the sofa, didn't stir as much as a whisker. At the other end of the same seat, however, a big white and orange cat sat up, because Tilly was a knowing cat awake to her mistress's rising tension.

'Oh, for goodness' sake!' Gigi gasped because nobody appeared to be chasing the foolish dog and, on that acknowledgement, she was already racing out of her front door to stage a rescue bid.

Well, you are a veterinary surgeon, she excused herself and, without hesitation, she plunged into the busy street where the animal was capering about, seemingly quite clueless as to the danger it was in from the car wheels, the shouts out of windows for it to move and the squealing horns. Not a street dog, no, someone's pet and more like a baby than a child with some common sense. Others might have turned their backs on such a view but not Gigi, who valued animals more than people.

Gigi had spent eighteen months living on the Greek island of Rhodes. She worked there at an animal rescue centre but had primarily come to Rhodes in the hope of actually getting to know the Greek half of her family. Basically, it hadn't worked out like that and her hopes and dreams had slowly withered. That ambition had, seemingly, been naïve. But then Gigi was accustomed to disillusionment when it came to family members. If her own mother hadn't had any time for her, why had she expected her father and her half-brothers to feel any different? Even so, she *had* got to know her Greek grandmother, Helene, and although Helene had passed away three months earlier, Gigi had got on well with the older woman and had also learned to speak fluent Greek. Two pluses, she told herself, but more negatives than pluses had featured in her family experiences.

As she filtered through traffic suddenly come to a standstill after two cars collided trying to avoid the dog, she realised that the foolish animal had got its long fragile tail locked between the cars. As a spate of furious Greek male voices broke out over the accident, Gigi pointed out the dog's predicament but, evidently, nobody cared enough to help her free the dog. She pushed at the cars, trying to move them even an inch to free the animal and then both male drivers started to shout at her about daring to try and intervene on behalf of the dog. Meanwhile the dog started frantically licking her bare legs as if he knew she was striving to save him and a woman got out of one of the stalled vehicles to help her. But Gigi had managed to get that tiny bit of trapped tail released even if, in doing so, she had scraped her knee painfully and hurt her wrist. Thanking the woman for coming to assist her, she smiled even though blood was running down her calf, and hastened back to the house to treat the dog's injury.

'Oh, you're just gorgeous and a total pet,' she told the dog cheerfully and he bounced up on his hind legs like an acrobat, a couple of feet taller than she was because now she could see that he was an Irish wolfhound about three feet tall when on four legs. Huge but a fine specimen of an animal, pedigreed and wearing what looked like an expensive collar. She'd bet he was microchipped, which she would check out at the rescue shelter first thing in the morning, so that she could restore him to his probably very grateful owner. But first, he needed his tail treated before the wound turned into something more serious.

'And you probably won't like me so much by the time I'm finished,' she warned him as she fetched her vet bag. 'Oh, and you've scraped your poor leg too. Mo. Is that your name or your owner's name?' It was picked out in sparkly stones on the collar. 'That's a very girly collar, Mo, for a big boy like you.'

Mo was a pushover of a dog. He lay down for her, seeming to instantly recognise a sympathetic audience. He allowed her to clean his tail and even his leg, which required several stitches. He didn't even object when she fitted a surgical collar on him to ensure that he left his injuries alone and didn't lick at them and irritate them more.

'Oh, I wish you were a street dog I could keep,' she sighed as she fed and watered him and walked him until he eventually, tiring of his adventures, folded down at her feet and went to sleep like a total babe. 'What a wonderful temperament you have!'

Some time during the night Mo padded upstairs, and Gigi shifted in the early hours and saw a pair of adoring brown eyes beside her on her bed. 'Today we find your owner and take you home,' she told him regretfully.

Not noticeably impressed by that announcement, Mo

went back to sleep, taking up more space on the bed than Gigi had for herself. 'You are a spoilt-rotten dog,' she told him ruefully.

He stuck to her like glue while she fed and walked him. She was about to head to her car to take him straight to work with her when she recalled that she had left her vet bag in her house. Although it wasn't *her* house, she reminded herself darkly, not with the big For Sale sign that had been fixed to it the week before. It was Helene's house and now her father's family were understandably keen to sell it, which was why she had decided to return to the UK with her pets as soon as she could make the arrangements. As she strolled back down the street, she noticed a crowd of men standing outside her door and banging the knocker as if someone's life depended on it.

'What on earth's going on?' she demanded, trudging through the clique of hovering men in dark suits.

'Mo!' a male voice cried with enthusiasm.

Mo reacted not at all. He licked Gigi's thigh ingratiatingly and did not budge an inch.

'What the hell have you done to him?' the same voice demanded thunderously. 'He's been hurt...*injured*!'

Gigi stuck her key in the front door and moved inside, Mo accompanying her. 'When I've checked out his microchip you can have him back...but not before. He hasn't even greeted you, which is weird when you're claiming to be his owner—'

'How *dare* you?' he demanded even louder.

'No, how dare you when I rescued this poor dog from traffic and treated him?' Gigi shot back at him without hesitation. 'That does not give you the right to come here and *shout* at me, you ignorant pig!'

To say that Jace was unaccustomed to such cavalier treatment from a woman would not have been an exaggeration. His jaw literally dropped as he gazed down at her, having already noticed that she had not deigned to look at *him* even once. And there she was, some impossibly tiny woman with a long, messy mop of brownish blonde hair, wearing shorts and a camisole like a...well, not like a streetwalker, he adjusted, for there was nothing come-hitherish about that outfit, nothing decorative or sexy. But she had stunning legs, he had noticed as she'd sauntered down the street with *his* dog. Mo was the one soft spot in Jace's hard heart. Hearing that Mo had broken free and run away while Jace was attending the funeral had sent him mad with worry.

'Treated him? How could *you* treat him?' Jace demanded, wishing that she would look up at him and behave more normally.

'I'm a veterinary surgeon, you dummy, and I'm not handing this beautiful dog back to you until you *prove* that he belongs to you. If you must, you can come inside and I'll explain what happened to him, but I should add that I have to be at work soon.'

'I thought he'd been kidnapped. There's a tracker on his collar—'

'He should be microchipped,' Gigi told him reprovingly as she stepped through her front door. 'That would be safer. I mean, what happens if the collar falls off or is removed? You couldn't find him then. Anyway, why would you stick a tracker on a dog, for goodness' sake?'

Jace breathed in deep and slow, as if he was bracing himself. What a weird woman—what a thoroughly weird woman! And then she finally paid him the compliment of looking up at him and he saw her for the first time…and she was gorgeous in that strangely natural way only a very few women could match. No make-up, nothing enhanced. Just pale porcelain skin, huge cornflower-blue eyes and a mouth, a sultry pink full mouth that could only exist for sin.

'Well. Come in if you're coming,' she told him impatiently. 'And I'm sorry but your friends will have to stay outside because it is a very small house and one stranger at a time is quite enough for me at this time of day.'

Dark colour edged Jace's cheekbones. A woman had never addressed him in that no-nonsense tone in his life. It felt exceedingly…wrong, he decided, wondering why she was reacting that way to him. Of course he had been rude, he reminded himself, attacking rather than pausing to first discover what had happened to his pet.

'Sit down,' Gigi urged. 'I'd offer you a coffee but I haven't got the time to entertain you right now—'

'Of course not,' Jace conceded, reeling back from her apparent indifference to him.

'Well, *sit*!' she shot at him. 'I can't abide someone so

tall standing over me all the time and talking down to me like I'm a child!'

Gigi sat down on the sofa. Mo climbed up beside her and, beneath his owner's incredulous gaze, reclined across the entire top of her like the little lap dog he so obviously wasn't and could never be, not when he was the size of a pit pony.

'You're unusually small,' Jace pointed out almost apologetically.

'*So?*' Gigi replied shortly.

Gigi surveyed the big powerful male with the bad temper and no manners. He looked rich, sophisticated, everything she was not. He was also as impossibly hand-some as a movie star. He didn't look quite real to her, seated as he was in Helene's former armchair in the very ordinary little sitting room.

Gigi told him in a few words about how she had seen Mo from her front window and how he had caused an accident and got his tail and his leg hurt. She explained her treatment much as if he were a potential adopter of an animal at the rescue shelter.

'Are you satisfied he wasn't being kidnapped now?' she enquired very drily.

'I apologise for that. I was upset, *worried* about him,' he stressed.

'Yes, you do leap to conclusions fast,' she conceded with a slight wrinkling of her delicious little nose. 'Per-haps I was a little hard on you. I'm not comfortable with volatile people.'

'What's your name?' Jace asked, relaxing a little from the sheer tension gripping him, a tension he couldn't even begin to understand beyond a barely acknowledged desire for her to like him.

'Gigi Campbell…and yours?'

Jace did not think he had had to introduce himself to a woman in living memory. It was unexpectedly refreshing. 'Jace Diamandis. You speak excellent Greek but going by your accent, you're *not* Greek—'

'No, I'm British…try and get your dog to come to you,' she urged, keen to get rid of him and get to work. 'I gather he's not microchipped? You should get that taken care of asap.'

'Tell me where you work and I'll take care of it,' Jace suggested in English.

'Yes, that would do,' Gigi conceded with innate practicality. 'Don't you realise that it's against the law *not* to have your dog microchipped? I work at a rescue shelter.'

Taken aback by that reproving response and casting a weathered eye at his dog, who had gone to sleep on his saviour's lap, Jace said, 'Let me take you to dinner this evening to thank you for rescuing him for me.'

'No need to put yourself to that trouble,' Gigi assured him cheerfully. 'I rescue animals all the time. It's my vocation.'

'I find that interesting. Taking you out for a meal would be a pleasure,' Jace asserted, wondering when she would crack and behave normally.

'Go on,' was all Gigi said in response. 'Try and get your dog to come to you…'

'Mo!' Jace grated.

Mo opened one eye, squinted at him and very carefully closed it again, playing dead.

'I think he's decided that he likes you better. He's not usually stubborn or disobedient,' Jace commented with a rare feeling of embarrassment, because he had owned the dog for two years and he was being royally ignored. 'I left him behind to attend a funeral yesterday and possibly he's sulking.'

'You'll have to carry him out then, because I *have* to get to work,' Gigi reminded him gently.

Jace sprang upright, opened her front door and two of the men left outside came in and carried a supine Mo out.

'Couldn't you have carried him yourself?' Gigi remarked in astonishment.

Faint colour flared along Jace's high cheekbones. She was the least tactful woman he had ever met, so why did he want her? And he did, he *knew* he did from the instant he had matched those legs to that beautiful heart-shaped face. Yet she wasn't even his type. He went for tall leggy blondes, not tiny, not impertinent, not anything other than conservative females. And this was a woman with a tortoise under her sofa, a bedraggled bird in a cage and a dog with one eye and three legs. Only the cat looked halfway normal in the assembly of animals. In fact, he didn't know what he was doing and it freaked him out more than a little. It was as if his brain went walkabout in front of her and he couldn't concentrate.

He would buy her flowers or something, forget about her because she didn't seem attracted to him in any way and that shocked him. In fact, it was the biggest shock Jace had withstood from a woman in many years.

There had been his best friend's wife, who had made a pass at him, all the employees over the years who had come on to him, every female student he had ever met. Jace had learned at a very early age that he was irresistible to her sex. He didn't kid himself that it was purely his looks and charm; he wasn't that innocent. No, it was literally the wealth and the lifestyle that made him so apparently irresistible to women.

'Thank you for looking after Mo,' he declared quietly. 'I truly appreciate your kindness.'

'Not a problem,' Gigi assured him, escorting him to the front door with enthusiasm.

'And if you should change your mind about dinner, here's my card.' Jace extended a business card to her. 'Maybe you have a boyfriend—'

Gigi raised both brows. 'Are you kidding? Men are more trouble than they're worth. I found that out years ago—'

'A girlfriend?' Jace persisted without even understanding why he was doing it, but he needed to know in that moment.

'Good heavens, no, I'm not gay, maybe just not that

interested in…er…dating or whatever,' she completed in an oddly embarrassed rush of self-defence.

Jace nodded and he didn't get it, he *still* didn't get it. He wanted to change her mind, but he didn't know enough about her or what was happening inside his own head to understand why she was virtually indifferent to him or why he didn't wish to accept that fact. He went back into the street and she slammed the door behind him as if he had been an unwelcome intrusion.

'A strange woman,' his chief of security commented.

'You have no idea,' Jace responded as a limo complete with a still snoozing Mo drew up at the pavement.

So strange that he couldn't take his eyes off her! All curves in a very small package, eyes as blue as the Greek sky, hair as streaky as toffee in a pan that he recalled from his childhood and the most flawless face and complexion. Shaking his black curly head at such peculiar thoughts, Jace got into the limo.

'You're a traitor, a turncoat,' he told his dog without hesitation. 'I've loved you for two years and you wouldn't give me as much as a tail wag when I came to fetch you home!'

Gigi went into work with relief.

'Thought you were planning to sleep in today,' Ioanna, the shelter nurse, quipped without much surprise at Gigi's appearance. 'You're a workaholic…admit it!'

'I couldn't sleep late today. I had a dog I found last night and he needed walking—'

'Gigi…you could go to a blasted pop concert and come home with a dog!' the older woman teased. 'But it's no life for someone your age.'

'I'm quite happy with my life as it is,' Gigi lied.

But she wasn't going to reference her experience of men to anyone she worked with. Even on Rhodes within her own family, she had learned how unreliable men were these days. She had three half-brothers who were man whores with tourists and one whose marriage had broken up because he had cheated on his wife. And what about her father, who had insisted he was legally separated from his wife at the time that Gigi was conceived? Gigi wasn't convinced of that legal-separation claim after meeting her father's wife, Katerina, who had treated her very much as though she were some designing young female trying to muscle in on *her* family.

Her mother had been a committed career woman, a high-earning nuclear physicist, who had travelled a lot, often working abroad on government projects. She had placed Gigi in boarding school at an early age to remain free of the domestic burden of raising a child. She had informed Gigi's father, Achilleus Georgiou, that she had had a child after their fling in Athens while she was in Greece at a conference. But Gigi's father had never bothered to come and visit Gigi or write to her or even contribute to her care.

Achilleus owned three thriving businesses in the Old Town and he had four sons, all of whom worked for him. Had Gigi paused to consider such hard, revealing facts she would not have been foolish enough to come to Greece in search of a family after her mother's sudden death. Unfortunately, she had decided to seek out her roots in the hope of making a connection, but it hadn't happened. She had simply met up with a bunch of uninterested people who had their own lives and didn't need her in those lives.

'So, tell me about the dog,' Ioanna encouraged.

And Gigi did, from start to finish when Mo had been carried out like a parcel and she had been invited yet again to dinner.

'So, why didn't you say yes? Was he ugly? Too old?'

'No...er...no, he was extremely good-looking, probably only a few years older than me, and he even gave me a business card.' Gigi giggled in recollection of that unexpected moment of formality and dug it out of the back pocket of her shorts with a flourish.

Ioanna snatched at the card and her eyes widened and her mouth fell open. '*Jace Diamandis*...oh, my word, I don't believe this!' she gasped. 'Only one of the richest men in the world! And certainly the richest in Greece!'

Gigi pursed her full pink lips. 'He did look kind of fancy—'

'*Fancy?* Haven't you noticed that giant matt-black yacht anchored out in the bay?' Ioanna practically shrieked in excitement. 'It belongs to him and the funeral he mentioned was his father's. He was buried yesterday.'

Gigi winced at that announcement, feeling that she

had signally failed to excuse Jace's loss of temper when it seemed he would naturally have been grieving. Poor guy, she thought helplessly, sympathetic for the first time towards her unwelcome visitor.

'And the worst thing of all is that you are not even impressed!' the nurse commented.

'Well, why would I be?' Gigi asked with a frown. 'What's his money got to do with me?'

'He asked you out and you said no! I can't believe that you said *no* to Jace Diamandis!'

'Well, he did seem a bit surprised that I was turning him down,' Gigi conceded reluctantly. 'But I got the impression that he was totally full of himself and that's a major turn-off for me. I wouldn't have had anything in common with him, so it would have been a waste of time meeting him again—'

'But you should have gone just for the *thrill*!' Ioanna carolled.

'I'm quite…shy with men. It wouldn't have worked and if he's that rich, it would have been just a plain peculiar experience. Look, who's first on today's surgical rota?' Gigi enquired, keen to get off the topic of Jace Diamandis and his filthy lucre and the unknown thrills he might be expected to offer.

On his legendary superyacht, *Sea King*, Jace was giving way to his curiosity and requesting an in-depth investigation into Gigi Campbell, who for some eccentric reason he couldn't get out of his head. He sent flowers too that evening when he assumed she would be at home.

Receiving a giant basket of glorious wildflowers absolutely bemused Gigi, who had never thought of herself as a flowery woman. She sat staring at them for almost an hour, and at the card, wondering what insanity had possessed Mo's owner. He was trying to say thank you, she supposed, failing to appreciate that she would have performed the same rescue bid on any animal running loose in busy traffic.

She wondered how Mo was getting on. She missed the dog. She had really, really liked Mo. Somehow, he had made her feel less lonely. She wondered if he performed the same service for Jace, but doubted that someone as handsome, powerful and wealthy could possibly feel in need of that kind of support.

On his yacht, Jace studied his disaffected dog, whimpering mournfully by the door as if he had been stolen against his will from Gigi, and he sighed heavily...

CHAPTER TWO

JACE THOUGHT UNUSUALLY hard about what he wore on the day he went to the rescue shelter. He ditched the designer business suits he invariably wore and picked jeans and a linen shirt, less formal, more approachable, he reasoned.

But *she* was all wrong for him, in any case, he reminded himself stubbornly. He had held a party the night before, a party attended by some very beautiful women, exquisitely dressed, flattering and polite women, and for the first time in his life, not one woman had appealed to his normally rampant libido. No, very weirdly, it was Gigi Campbell's image that he couldn't get out of his head. That truth was annoying the hell out of him. Was it the fact that she was a challenge? A challenge was something he had never met with in her sex. Could he possibly be *that* basic? He suppressed a cynical shudder at the suspicion.

At the rescue shelter, Gigi was attending to her usual duties without much concern. Ioanna might be champing at the bit for Jace Diamandis to come through the door for Mo's appointment to be microchipped but Gigi was not. In fact, with the vet nurse hanging about as if she were awaiting a visitation from a god amongst men, Gigi was more inclined to pity Jace for the excitement he seemed to engender in those who recognised his name. All the poor guy was doing was trying to get his dog microchipped. He had seemed shocked when she had mentioned that that, after all, was Greek law and it was a perfectly normal response for the man to attend to that oversight as soon as possible.

Even so, the prospect of his imminent appearance did fluster her a little and that bothered her. After all, she was a woman who had given up on men. One broken heart had been quite enough for her. Rory had cheated on her, blaming her for it because she had refused to give him her body, having known him only a few weeks. But in so doing, he had taught her a good lesson. She would never trust a member of the male sex again. They were all obsessed with sex and the number of women they could get into their beds. She was well aware though that there were women of the same ilk because she had known a couple like that at university, but the majority of her sex were a little less crude and more emotion-based than men.

'He's...*here*!' Ioanna squealed like a member of the Jace Diamandis fan club and Gigi said not a word, conscious that all the female shelter workers were equally enthralled and would be peering out of windows and hovering in doorways.

Gigi would not allow herself to look. For some peculiar reason, she *wanted* to look and that irritated her, particularly when his image was already stuck like glue inside her brain. The high sculpted cheekbones, the imperious ebony brows, the strong masculine nose, the wide sensual mouth. And the whole topped by the most gloriously cute glossy black curls, not to mention the unexpected eyes green as emeralds lighting up that lean dark face. Drop-dead gorgeous. Yes, Jace definitely had cornered the looks department with a meteoric score but, unfortunately, he knew that rather too well. As for his reputation? Well, that certainly didn't add to his image as a plus. She had seen enough online to decide that he was way out of *her* league.

'Good morning, Gigi,' Jace murmured perfectly politely while she busied herself rearranging the equipment she used, and she heard the faint strand of amusement edging his dark, deep voice.

'Good morning, Mr Diamandis...' she contrived to say flatly before she was unceremoniously engulfed by an ecstatic wolfhound who knocked her off her feet with enthusiasm.

'My apologies... I shouldn't have let him off the leash.' A lean strong hand closed over hers and virtually hauled her back upright from the floor, where she had fallen to her knees, while Mo tried to canter a circle round her in his excitement.

The warmth of his hand sent the most curious zing through her entire body and she glanced up at him, only to be consumed by the scorching flash effect of dancing emerald-green eyes. Her entire body heated up, her nipples prickling inside her bra, a sliding sensation tugging between her legs. Those feelings made her grit her teeth in annoyance and free her hand, which he was *still* holding, and drop back down to her knees again to give his dog her attention.

Jace wasn't accustomed to being blanked but he took it like a man, like a thrown gauntlet, because at the moment she had collided with his eyes, he had read her response as clearly as a shrieking alarm. The flush on her cheeks, her dilated pupils? Neither spoke of indifference. Gigi Campbell wanted him but at the same time she didn't *want* to want him, he recognised with satisfaction. He watched his dog fawn on her like a subservient slave. Indeed, he surveyed the delighted reunion with a curled lip of near disbelief because, in his experience, Mo was not that friendly an animal and rarely approached anyone else for attention. But Mo couldn't get enough of Gigi.

'Sorry about this,' Gigi said, unselfconsciously rising to her feet again with a final pat of Mo's head. 'But he's the most beautiful dog and *so* affectionate.'

'Is this…er…procedure likely to hurt him?' Jace enquired.

'For a split second…' Gigi wielded the tool and Mo stood like a statue for her, trying to lick at the knee that was all the skin he could reach below her lab coat. 'Stop that, Mo…'

The sunlight coming through the window lit up the blonde streaks in her light brown hair, settled lovingly on the porcelain-perfect skin of her profile, her slender neck, the thrust of her small firm breasts. Jace gritted his teeth because his body reacted like an adolescent's in her vicinity. That fast he was hard as a rock and it infuriated him, infuriated him in the only way it could a usually very controlled and reserved male. For the space of a timeless moment, he had been out of control, picturing her splayed across his bed like some kind of sexual sacrifice, picturing a *fantasy*. And Jace didn't have fantasies about women, had never had the need, had never wanted any woman that he hadn't had.

'There…that's done and, of course, you were a good boy,' Gigi told Mo, fondling his silky ears. 'Thank you for bringing him here so that I could see him again. I'm sure you could have sent him anywhere with an employee to have him microchipped.'

Yes, she knew who he was now, Jace savoured before it occurred to him that it had not changed her attitude one iota. She was rather more interested in his dog than she was in him.

'He may only have been with you one night but he formed an attachment to you,' Jace conceded.

'He slept with me. That's probably it. I didn't have the heart to put him back downstairs because he's *so* cuddly!' Gigi stooped to give another hug to Mo.

'You let him into your bed?' Jace elevated an ebony

brow. 'I wouldn't dream of allowing that. No wonder he got so attached!'

'Sorry for teaching him a bad habit.' Gigi laughed, a low husky laugh, animation skimming her lovely face, her blue eyes sparkling, her soft mouth smiling to reveal a slice of pearly teeth. For an instant, she simply took his breath away and all he wanted to do was kiss her. The strength of that impulse spooked him into swinging away to put some distance between them. It was as if she had shot him up with pure adrenaline.

'Where do I pay?' he asked her, turning back around to face her.

'We charge the basic rate at Reception outside. I guess that won't be a problem for you,' Gigi framed awkwardly, striving hard not to stare at him. But he was so good-looking he kept on stealing her attention like a sneak thief. And never mind his beautiful face. He had an even more beautiful body. Tall, lean, fit, narrow waist, taut hips, powerful thighs and biceps, long, straight legs. Discomfiture relating to those reflections sent colour flying into her cheeks as she clashed with his amused green gaze. She stiffened at the intensity and the fire she saw in that scrutiny. He had watched her checking him out. Unnerved by that awareness, she dropped her head again.

'When did you find out who I was?' Jace asked carelessly.

'My nurse recognised your name. I think there's another patient waiting,' she prompted him very quietly, too aware of his volatile nature to be as blunt as she had been at their first meeting.

Thee mou, she was trying to get rid of him again, Jake registered in consternation. 'Why won't you have dinner with me when you're attracted to me?'

Utterly thrown by that confident assurance that she was attracted to him and by his unexpected candour, Gigi froze in her movement towards the door. 'Maybe I don't see what we would have in common…and I'm not the sort of woman who's likely to sleep with you on a first date, so we'd both be wasting our time—'

Jace threw his handsome head back in disconcertion, surprised that she would be that blunt. 'Doesn't it occur to you that I may not be that predictable?'

'Your reputation suggests that you're *very* predictable.'

'You think it's fair to judge me on the stories other people tell about me?' Jace lanced back at her a tinge harshly. 'I live in a goldfish bowl—'

'And you're very visible in it,' Gigi said in what she hoped was a soothing tone. 'But I *wasn't* judging you. Your life is none of my business—'

'Maybe I *want* you to make it your business,' Jace shot back at her without hesitation.

And Gigi almost laughed but dared not because he was acting defensively. But she was tempted to laugh at the concept of a guy with private jets, yachts and the like taking a genuine interest in a hard-working veterinary surgeon without an ounce of glamour. 'OK. I need to get back to work, Jace. There's a full waiting room out there.'

A stony aspect turned his carved jawline to granite. In silence he nodded, attached Mo's leash again and strode out. Jace had never been so conscious that he wanted to smash something with violence. His temper had rocketed up like lava in a volcano but he refused to show it around her when she had already labelled him' volatile'. And he wasn't volatile, not remotely volatile, he assured himself fiercely. He wasn't thinking that way because he wasn't accustomed to criticism, either. He had excellent relationships with his staff...*didn't he*?

She had blown him off *twice*. On one level he couldn't believe it, on another he was all the more determined to catch her. The investigation report hadn't come back yet. He wanted to know what the name Gigi was short for. He wanted to know what age she was. He wanted to know every damned thing there was to know about her!

But wasn't it a little unhinged to still be so interested in a woman after she had turned him down? An uneasy touch of ice trickled down Jace's rigid spine at that lowering apprehension. He would put her behind him, forget about her. Some strange notion had brought him back to her again and now he regretted it. Although it went against the grain to admit it, Gigi had been right: what did they have in common? And he would've only spent one night with her, in any case. It was insane to rate one woman any higher than the rest of the female sex, crazy to believe there could be some more special woman out there for him, especially when he was the last guy alive to want that *one* special woman.

Inside the shelter, Gigi's thoughts were travelling in the opposite direction. Possibly she had grown too rigid about protecting herself from predatory men, she was thinking abstractedly. And that very abstraction bothered her because no male had ever stuck around inside her head but Jace. Only wasn't she being a bit juvenile and hysterical saying no to a mere dinner invitation because he attracted her? So, she had got hurt before but sooner or later everyone got hurt in affairs of the heart. One person wanted one thing, the other something else. That was simply life and she had already warned him in advance that she wouldn't be inviting him into her bed.

Two days later, leash trailing again, Mo was sleeping on Gigi's doorstep when she arrived home. 'Oh, you bad dog,' she said very softly, stroking a silky ear while she considered the awkward prospect of having to phone Jace to tell him that his dog was with her again. She dug out his card.

'You've got him, haven't you?' Jace interrupted within seconds of her beginning to speak.

'Yes, sorry about that. He was waiting at my front door when I got home—'

'I wouldn't have believed that he could have retraced his steps from the harbour to your house last week. I'll collect him...or I'll have him collected—'

'Jace?' she broke in. 'I'll agree to dinner.'

A stark little silence fell.

'I'll send a car for you—'

'To go where?'

'You are so distrustful,' Jace complained.

'Merely mindful of my safety.'

'My yacht, *Sea King*—'

'I'd prefer a public place,' she said apologetically.

'Would you also enjoy the paparazzi surrounding us? That's what happens in public places when I'm visible,' Jace told her drily.

'OK, the yacht,' she conceded reluctantly, definitely not wishing to appear in newsprint in his company because she took her anonymous life for granted.

'Eight,' he specified.

'Eight-thirty,' she told him. 'I have to walk both dogs.'

And then the call ended without another word.

Well, did you expect him to turn verbal wheelies at the end of the line when you finally agreed? Blinking, already wondering if she had made an unwise decision, Gigi set down her phone.

She went for a shower before taking a simple electric-blue maxi, sleeveless dress from her wardrobe. Her first summer in Rhodes she had assumed she would have more of a social life with her Greek family and she had extended her very practical wardrobe. But in actuality she had received few invitations. Everybody had been keen to meet her once out of curiosity, but their interest hadn't gone much deeper than that. Maybe if there had been a half-sister, *she* would have been more interested,

only, knowing her luck, Gigi conceded ruefully, a potential half-sister would have been furious to discover
that her father had a second daughter.

A limousine drew up at her door, paying no attention
whatsoever to the 'no parking' lines. Gigi stepped out
straight away, Mo walking by her side. She would've
insisted on driving her own car to the harbour had it not
occurred to her that trying to squeeze Mo into her tiny
two-door car might make the big dog baulk. He stepped
up onto the luxurious back seat beside her and flopped
his head down on her lap for her to pat. 'Life's so much
simpler for you,' she sighed.

Either the huge yacht had an enormous crew or it
seemed as though an awful lot of them were curious
about Jace's visitor because every direction Gigi looked
in there seemed to be a face peering at her, and the cap-
tain, wearing his official uniform, greeted her as though
she were arriving royalty when she stepped off the motor
launch that had whisked her from the harbour. That welcome, along with the opulence surrounding Gigi, just
about deprived her of breath. She emerged from a lift
into a vast reception area.

Clearly designed for his parties.

She was offered a drink by a stewardess who could
have featured in a Miss World competition.

Does he perve on his staff?

Stop it, Gigi warned herself, you're being judgmental
on nothing more than the headlines he attracts.

'Gigi. Sorry not to be here to greet you,' Jace intoned as he strode through an archway. 'I was taking a call.'

For a split second, she felt as though her heart stopped beating and the world suddenly swam into sharper focus on his lean dark face. Green eyes flaring like fireworks, startlingly intense and potent. It shook her up. She stole a fast glance at him and then walked over to the windows as if she were examining the fabulous view of the harbour and the winding road beyond it. She spun back, her heart now beating at an accelerated rate, and watched Mo trot over to greet Jace as normally as if the dog had just entered the room rather than run off on his owner again.

'I think, as far as he's concerned, *he* was retrieving *you*,' Jace quipped as though he had been thinking the exact same thing.

'Probably,' she agreed with a slightly nervous laugh.

'What do you like to eat?'

'I eat virtually everything, and I have no allergies.'

'Gigi…what's that short for? Or is it only a nickname?' he heard himself ask, startling himself with the level of his curiosity about her.

'It says Giselle on my birth certificate, so it must be my mother who shortened it because I've never been called anything else…or maybe it was one of the nannies who looked after me.'

'You were raised by nannies?'

'Yes, until I went to boarding school.' Gigi's eyes stung on the thought that she knew very little about her earliest years because Nadine Wilson had never been a sentimental parent, delighted to recall her daughter's babyhood. In the same way there were only a handful of photos of her between birth and starting school and some of them were on medical records.

'And after that?' Jace prompted, wondering why the hell he was still being so nosy.

'My mother sometimes worked abroad so for term breaks I often went to friends' houses or on study trips, which suited me the best. I was a nerd from day one at school,' she admitted calmly. 'There's lots of programmes out there for nerdy kids. Occasionally a short-term nanny would be hired but usually the housekeeper was capable of looking out for me.'

'There you are…we *do* have something in common,' Jace declared with satisfaction. 'Nannies and boarding schools. My parents were busy people too.'

A little uneasy below that shimmering emerald-green appraisal, Gigi parted her lips. 'You mentioned food…'

Recalled by the reminder that she had only just arrived and he had been interrogating her, faint colour enhanced Jace's high cheekbones. 'You can literally have anything you like because I have a team of chefs in the galley.'

'That's good. I find cooking a chore,' she confided lightly. 'It's a struggle to remind myself that I should eat a healthy meal when the easy options are often unhealthy. I'll have a Greek salad and…er stuffed veggies?'

'No appetiser?'

'Not for me. I'm not a big eater but feel free on your own behalf,' she urged, a little flushed as she sipped at her orange juice and sat down at the side of the polished dining table in the indicated seat across from his.

'I'm attempting to replicate the restaurant experience I denied you…and you won't allow me to do it,' Jace reproved.

'I guess that's because I'm really wondering what I'm doing here with you,' Gigi admitted frankly.

Jace gritted his teeth. 'Don't start that again.'

He snapped his fingers and the stewardess appeared to take their order. Apart from an aside to check that she wasn't vegetarian, he ordered food she hadn't requested and wine.

'I don't really drink,' she told him in a small voice.

Jace shot her a dazzling smile. 'No worries. I do.'

That smile made every cell in her body sit up and take notice. She simply stared back at him for a moment, mesmerised by that outpouring of charm but distrusting him all the more.

'What are you so scared of?' Jace asked her almost lazily, his bright green eyes suddenly as shrewd as cutting knives. 'Has some guy in the past assaulted you?'

'No!'

'That's how you come across,' Jace murmured. 'I assure you that I have never laid a single finger on an unwilling woman.'

Gigi's flush had spread as far as her hairline. Indeed she felt as if she were being boiled alive with mortification inside her own skin. 'That's…er good to know,' she mumbled. 'No, I don't date or anything because I've rarely felt the need to do so. I did once a couple of years ago but he turned out to be a loser and that put me off—'

'*Once?* You're *that* easily put off?'

'You wouldn't understand—'

'Why wouldn't I understand?'

'You're an extrovert. I'm an introvert. I internalise stuff. Socially I'm a wallflower. I've always been that way.'

A lean brown hand came down to where her smaller hand was trembling and covered it with sudden warmth. 'It's all right to be who you are. There's nothing wrong with that. Stop apologising for it,' he urged, startling her with both those words and that physical gesture. 'Don't overthink this. It's only a meal—'

'On a freaking yacht!' she shot back at him with a choking giggle.

'On a freaking yacht,' conceded Jace, still smiling as he collided with those superb cornflower-blue eyes of hers. 'And you want to know why you're here? You're absolutely beautiful and I can't push you out of my head. It's like you've taken up residence there and I can't see anyone else and it's driving me crazy!'

As his dark deep drawl rose a little at the end of that final, disconcerting admission, Gigi's extreme tension gave and she suddenly smiled and relaxed. 'Same here.'

Jace dealt her a mock-stunned appraisal, his forceful gaze flaming over her. 'Are you seriously admitting that?'

Gigi nodded gravely. 'But what's the point—?'

'No...*no*,' Jace cut in with ruthless cool. 'Stop with the negatives. Slow that busy brain of yours. Enjoy the evening.'

Gigi knew that she suffered from a lot of negative self-talk but that underlying anxiety had always been with her. Her mother had been a very outgoing person and her daughter's different nature had offended her expectations. 'You talk sense,' she said, 'and that surprises me.'

Jace laughed out loud, amused by her ignorance. 'Gigi... I'm the CEO of a very large group of companies. Of course I've got sense.'

'Obviously I read the wrong stuff online when I looked you up.' Gigi frowned on her own behalf. 'I read the gossip. There's no real excuse for that.'

'In your position, I would probably have done the same. I came back onboard here and asked for a private investigator to check you out for me,' Jace admitted. 'And he still can't get back to me. He can't trace you, for some reason.'

Gigi was studying him wide-eyed and then she laughed with unmistakable amusement. 'I had to change my surname to my grandmother's to inherit her estate. That's my mother's mother. She never forgave my mother for falling pregnant outside marriage and she never asked to meet me, but she still put me in her will.

That was a huge surprise. Growing up, my surname was Wilson because my mother was briefly married and divorced when she was quite young and she changed her name. Becoming a Campbell to match my grandmother meant that I could pay off my student loans, which was *huge* for me at the time.'

'I thought you'd be angry when I told you about the investigation I ordered on you—'

Below his arrested gaze, Gigi shrugged a slight shoulder. 'I guess that's your equivalent of the online snooping session that I did. I'm not annoyed but then I've got nothing I feel the need to hide.'

The first course arrived at the table. She ate with unusual appetite, savouring every tiny bite. Somehow, and she had completely no idea *how*, Jace had enabled her to relax in his presence for the first time. He made easy conversation. He was very polite. He was amazingly comfortable to be with. An enigma, she decided, seemingly quite unlike his glitzy playboy image. Or was she falling for an act? She suppressed that suspicion, scolding herself for that less than positive thought. Why would someone as rich and good-looking as Jace Diamandis go to so much trouble for someone like her if he *weren't* genuinely interested?

Jace whipped his hand from Gigi's only when he realised that he had retained his hold on those slender fingers. He was still recovering from the shock value of having told her that he couldn't get her out of his head. Never before had he been guilty of going in keen with a woman, because it handed out the wrong message and it wasn't fair…even if it was true? Every glimpse he got of her stuck to him like superglue.

Possibly that was the challenge she seemed to be for him. His intentions were wholly basic as usual, he reassured himself. A good time would be enjoyed by both of them; however, it wouldn't be heading beyond the bedroom door in any direction. No offence intended, no harm done, surely? So, why was he feeling like a bastard all of a sudden? Admittedly she was a sensitive woman and he didn't have a sensitive bone in his entire body. At least, he never had with anyone else. Why the hell was he even thinking along such complex lines?

'You seem preoccupied,' Gigi remarked, because he had been staring at her with brooding intensity.

'It's you…you preoccupy me.'

'That's a compliment, *isn't it*?'

'A foe worthy of my mettle,' Jace teased helplessly, because he could scarcely tell her the truth that being so drawn to her made him feel slightly on the edge of insane.

The main course arrived. He asked her about her animals and she worked through them one by one.

'How on earth could that little tortoise be too large for its owner?' Jace demanded.

'Because they got him when he was teeny-tiny and probably put him in an aquarium or something to keep him and he outgrew his space. I'm planning to let Humphrey go free when I find the right setting for him,' she explained. 'But he has to learn how to forage for himself before I can do that and he's pretty hopeless at the minute. He's very lazy—'

'Give him a break. Maybe the aquarium was very small,' Jace suggested seriously.

And Gigi laughed. 'You know, looking at your fancy suit, I would never have guessed it, but you genuinely do like animals.'

'Yes. Mo the defector who wants to exchange me for you isn't much of an advertisement in that line.'

'No, he loves you. I just think he's not used to female attention—'

'I'd like to think that, but there are several female crew members who like him and he's never gone missing to find them.'

Jace thrust back his chair with sudden restiveness. 'Let me give you a tour of the yacht and when we come back the last course will be waiting. Do you want coffee?'

'Tea's more my speed at this hour but I always sleep like a log anyway,' she conceded absently.

Not in my bed, you won't, Jace promised himself soothingly because he knew she was a very poor bet from his point of view.

She was clever but there was not the smallest attempt to hook him in her appearance or her behaviour and he wasn't stupid. The modest dress, the lack of cosmetics, the absence of flirtation. Right now, Gigi was merely tolerating him. He would probably have to fill

out a thirty-page questionnaire before she would consider sliding between those sheets with him. She wasn't
a woman likely to take a risk on him or one likely to
succumb to temptation. She liked security, familiarity,
safe bets and he offered none of those things. And yet it
was strangely relaxing to be in her company, regardless
of the reality that sex wasn't on the immediate agenda,
possibly even because of that fact. Her lack of expectations and her sheer honesty were soothing.

'You're so different from me—'

'Stop building more walls between us,' Jace urged,
exasperated at the manner in which she continually
stepped further away from him, reinforcing her apparent
conviction that they could never be together in any way.
He swore to himself that he would teach her otherwise.

'Is that what I'm doing?'

Shimmering green eyes as bright as jewels in sunshine assailed her. 'You know you are.'

Gigi went pink and felt exposed as the unexciting
woman she believed she was.

Jace wondered when he had last, if ever, been with a
woman who blushed. Next time he met a woman who
blushed he should walk the other way fast, he instructed
himself. 'You haven't mentioned a father yet—'

'And you haven't mentioned a single word about your
background,' she reminded him as he flung open the
door on a plush cinema room and moved on to show
her a gym.

'Most people already know all about me,' he declared.

'My mother died when I was six and when she was in the act of leaving my father for another man. She crashed her car with her lover. Both of them died. Thankfully she hadn't taken me with her.'

But his lean, strong features were taut as elastic pulled too tight and she grasped that it wasn't that simple for him. He might be grateful that he hadn't died in the same crash but he was still hurt that his mother had left him behind.

By instinct, in the same way she absently fondled Mo's ears as he walked with them, she closed a hand over Jace's fist. No, sophisticated he might be, but he wasn't good at hiding his emotions. But then few hot-blooded temperaments were, she reflected. 'That must've been tough.'

'No,' he disagreed. 'It got tough when my father decided that he couldn't stand the sight of me because I looked so like my mother and sent me and the nanny to live with my grandparents. And my grandfather was too ill to want to take on the burden of a young child.'

Her heart smote her for him. Gigi had always had a very soft heart and what had been done to Jace when he was a young child drove a compassionate knife through her chest. He had been rejected by his family and to some degree the same thing had happened to her. Her mother had raised her, feeding, clothing and educating her, but she had not loved her or looked for her when she wasn't there.

'What?' Jace chided. 'No words of wisdom now?'

'You don't like talking about it and I perfectly understand that and won't mention it again. However, don't get sarky,' Gigi warned him, removing her fingers from his.

'There *was* a happy ending,' Jace heard himself expand, missing that innocent physical contact with her and furious about the fact. 'My father's youngest brother and his husband offered me a home a few weeks later at a family meeting. Everyone was very grateful for that solution because my father was king in the family and nobody wanted me in the same household lest he stop visiting or favouring them.'

'And your father's brother?'

'He wasn't financially dependent on my father while the others were. He and Marcus are partners in a chain of very successful European art galleries. I was very lucky that they wanted me,' he breathed stiffly as she looked up at him, her wonderful eyes intent, her entire posture leaning in towards him in what he interpreted as an invitation.

Jace trailed a lean forefinger slowly up her arm, savouring the goose bumps that followed in the wake of his touch. He reached her delicate collarbone and traced it as well. Unlike him, she was slight in build, shockingly fragile to the feel.

'Jace…?' she whispered shakily.

And, like a male going for a gold medal, he tasted her soft, pouting lips gently and her head swam as if she had taken alcohol, a strange breathless weakness engulfing her as butterflies unfurled low in her tummy. He deepened the pressure and closed his arms round her without warning and just as quickly he was devouring her mouth as if he couldn't get enough of her.

And that was fine, she acknowledged dimly in the very midst of that hot, explosive kiss, because she couldn't get enough of him either. Her arms came up and closed on his broad shoulders as she stretched herself up to him, wishing she had worn heels. His tongue delved in her mouth and she shivered against him with sensation. It was like standing in a force ten gale. It was dynamite, everything she had ever hoped to feel and never found. There was no fumbling, no unease. It was as though her body had been waiting for Jace Diamandis all her life…

Both of them breathless, he pulled back from her and continued the tour, only this time around he kept a hold of her hand, reinstating that connection even when she had to step away.

CHAPTER THREE

GIGI LOOKED UP at Jace in the moonlight. His lean, hard-boned features were contemplative as the motor launch whizzed them back to the harbour. A phalanx of security staff ringed them because Jace did not like to be photographed against his will and had what struck her as an almost paranoiac need to ensure that his movements remained undocumented by the paparazzi.

Without warning, he folded both arms round her, pulling her close to the heat and solidity of his long lean length, and reaction went running through her like a crazy song rising in volume inside her. It touched every part of her. Her heart skipped a beat. Her nipples tightened almost painfully and there was a clenching low in her feminine core. Butterflies danced in her tummy. Concentration became a huge challenge.

'We're alone,' he insisted, against all the evidence to the contrary.

Gigi didn't want him to kiss her with so many men standing around, even though it was true that all of them were carefully looking in other directions. 'This is weird,' she hissed up at him, small hands braced and

spread across his wide chest to forge some distance between them. 'You should've stayed on the yacht—'

'Didn't want to part with you yet,' he growled.

'You're seeing me in the morning,' she reminded him
unevenly, her voice slipping and slurring as she collided
with his intent gaze, the greenness blacked out by the
low light but the expression no less forceful.

'You should've stayed on the yacht—'

'I have pets to look after,' she reminded him yet
again, one hand sliding up off his chest onto a wide
hard shoulder as she looked up him.

'I could've had that handled for you—'

'You're like a toddler sometimes!' she whispered in
sudden frustration, leaning close to his ear. 'If you can't
get your own way, you get angry—'

'I'm not getting angry,' Jace grated between evenly
clenched white teeth and it was the biggest lie he had
ever told, but he was damned if he was about to qualify
for that demeaning 'volatile' label again. People who
couldn't control their emotions, like his father, who had
rejected him, like his mother, who had put her love life
ahead of her son, often made mistakes they couldn't
come back from. He had no plans to ever make those
kinds of mistakes.

Her free hand mock-punched him on the chest. '*And*
you're such a liar!' she countered in another tone entirely, a forgiving tone of understanding, because she
had had to fight herself to walk away from him too.

And that had shaken Gigi deep, shaken her up, shaken

her inside out because she had never felt anything like the connection she felt with Jace with any other man. He felt like something in her bones, something familiar and, oh, so precious and that was exhilarating but it was also terrifying. No matter what she felt, she didn't *know* him or, at least, she hadn't known him long enough. She didn't want to rush into anything with him. She needed to step back, take a breath and work out if it would be sensible to move forward. Her disillusionment on the family front had taught her to protect herself before she risked her heart.

'You're busy thinking of all the reasons why you shouldn't be with me,' Jace intoned knowingly in her ear as he bent his handsome dark head. 'Why do you think I tried to keep you onboard, even in another bed?'

Even the way he said that word 'bed' set her alight somewhere deep down in her body and she quivered, tapped out on words of wisdom, vaguely accepting that she was on her own with no guidance or easy solution to so powerful an attraction. It was intimidating that he knew what she was thinking almost before she thought it. 'Tomorrow,' she told him steadily, suddenly proud that she had retained that much resistance to a male she found virtually irresistible.

'Tomorrow,' Jace repeated in another tone entirely, his hungry mouth claiming hers with fierce hunger, his tongue delving deep, twining with hers, and her hands gripped his forearms to steady her stance because her knees were weak. And nobody had ever kissed her the way Jace kissed her, as if 'tomorrow' were a hundred years away.

He drew back from her and that was when she realised that the launch had already docked and that everyone onboard was looking to Jace to issue instructions. Her face burned as though hellfire had flamed beneath her skin and she lifted her head high as Jace handed her off the craft and she stepped down onto the dock, accompanied to the car that awaited her. Jace lived in another world, totally another world from hers and one with different rules and dangers. She refused to look back at him even though she knew he was still watching her and she breathed in deep and long to regain her calm. Unfortunately, when it came to her reaction to Jace, he had the same effect on her as an explosive device thrown into a tranquil pond.

Back home, sliding into bed for what little remained of the night, she was too tired to agonise and she slept almost as soon as her head hit the pillow.

First thing, she was too busy to think about anything other than the needs of her pets and getting to work for the short surgery she offered on Saturday mornings. She worked for a charity but she didn't get paid for Saturday mornings when she volunteered her services for those who could not afford to pay for treatment from more expensive places. Only when she was hurriedly packing a bag for the rest of her day did she allow her thoughts to stray to Jace.

About the last thing she was expecting at nine o'clock

on a Saturday was a very loud rat-a-tat-tat on the front door knocker. And opening the door to find her Greek father and her four half-brothers waiting there was an even bigger shock. 'Has something happened?'

Achilleus Georgiou stepped through the door with a thunderous expression. 'Yes, something has happened,' he said very drily, extending a newspaper to her like exhibit A in a murder trial.

Frowning, Gigi peered and then her face lit up pink in mortification. In spite of all Jace's precautions, there they were in print on the launch kissing and there was another much clearer photo of her face as she stepped off the launch at the marina. Then and there, she scolded herself for assuming that Jace's concern about the paparazzi was paranoid. Evidently someone with a long-distance telephoto lens had spotted and caught them together.

'How did you meet him?' one of her four half-brothers demanded, all five men standing around her looking annoyed and accusing.

'I met him when I saved his dog from getting run over on the road outside,' Gigi advanced quietly. 'What's it to you?'

'What's it to any of us?' another half-brother piped up in apparent wonderment at her attitude. 'You're making an exhibition of yourself with a guy no decent woman would associate with!'

'Is that so?'

'Yes, I'm sorry to say it is,' her father stepped in to

LYNNE GRAHAM   55

confirm. 'Diamandis has an appalling reputation with women but possibly you were not aware of that fact?'

Achilleus had the brass to look hopeful as he asked that question and Gigi squared her slight shoulders. 'No. I read about his reputation online—'

'Then why the hell—?'

'Are you crazy?'

'What man will want you after he's ditched you and moved on?'

'You're soiling the Georgiou family name!'

As that storm of male protest was unleashed on her, Gigi stood even taller. 'But I'm *not* a Georgiou. And I'm *not* a member of your family.'

'You are my daughter!' her father proclaimed.

'You are our sister!'

Gigi reckoned that it was most unfortunate that they had never once uttered such keen sentiments over the past eighteen months when she had hung around on the edge of their family group, unaccepted, never once sought out. No, she had arranged every meeting between them all, each and every one. And many of those encounters had taken place only because Helene had still been alive and, naturally, they had wished to visit *her*, their sick grandmother, with whom Gigi had lived.

'Ask your sons to leave,' she told her father. 'I will talk to you, nobody else.'

Her half-brothers shuffled out looking upset and angry at her apparent lack of understanding of their feelings.

'I can see that this is an intervention,' Gigi said quietly when she was finally alone with the older man. 'And doubtless well intended to protect me, but I'm a woman of twenty-three years of age and an independent adult. I do as I like and I don't wish to be in conflict with you but you have *never* been a father to me.'

'I'm sorry but I was worried about you. You're on your own. He's a womaniser and I don't want to see you getting hurt.' With this little unexpected admission, Achilleus backed off a step, his weathered but still attractive face a mask of guilt and disconcertion, and her kind heart smote her because he was not a man capable, it seemed, of sharing his feelings, of admitting what had actually happened between her mother and him. Her mother had refused to talk about that as well. He was an old-school man of a different generation, but he had had months to bring himself to that point of talking about what mattered most and he still hadn't done it, still hadn't grasped that nettle. Yet in spite of those facts, he had still somehow decided that he had the right to come to her and criticise her conduct as though he were a true father to her. That admission that he was genuinely worried about her getting hurt, however, took the edge off her irritation. I'm sorry,' She sighed. 'I'm all grown now. Nobody tells me what to do. I'm single and so is Jace. If he were a married man or engaged in criminal activities, I could understand your objections, but not in these circumstances. From what I hear, he is a perfectly respectable businessman—a very rich one, I will agree, but nonetheless there's nothing dodgy about him.'

'For your sake, I hope that is true,' Achilleus said anxiously. 'But he does have an unsavoury reputation with your sex, and you have never impressed me as the kind of ambitious woman who seeks a jet-set lifestyle.'

'I'm not but I like Jace,' Gigi responded. 'I'm not expecting a for ever and ever happy ending with him either, but I will continue to see him…for the present.'

Achilleus dipped his head a shade in grudging acceptance of her adult status and added very awkwardly, 'I wish it had been possible for things to be different between us—'

Gigi flinched. 'It could have been different but nobody made the effort,' she pointed out ruefully.

The older man turned his head away, his discomfiture palpable, and a few minutes later he was gone, refusing a cup of coffee while ignoring the opportunity to put their relationship on a firmer, closer basis. She thought it ironic that her entire Greek family had landed on her doorstep at an early hour when they decided that she had done something wrong but that the same family had been wholly uninterested in treating her like a daughter or a sister beforehand. It hurt, but not as much as their indifference had hurt eighteen months earlier when she was still all bright-eyed and bushy-tailed optimistic about developing those relationships. In spite of that, however, she felt better for having spoken up in her own defence and laid down boundaries. She had stood up for herself, said what she had to say without apology and that could only be a sensible move.

She went into work, relieved that there was no sign she had been identified by the paparazzi as Jace's companion. No, she was a mystery woman and, hopefully, she would remain one. That hope was crushed the instant Ioanna raced into the surgery to join her on a day that she did not usually work. 'So, tell all!' she vented straight off.

'You recognised me,' Gigi gathered with a frown.

'It's a very good photo. Everyone here recognised you,' Ioanna confirmed to her dismay. 'Someone somewhere will talk and you'll be identified…there's nothing surer.'

Gigi texted Jace that she would drive herself to the marina and she ignored his objections when she left the surgery, climbing into her tiny car with Hoppy and refusing to be menaced by invisible photographers out to make money out of her image. As a result she bore a closer resemblance to a bag lady than a woman Jace would date. Hair in a high ponytail, she wore sweatpants and an oversized hoodie in spite of the heat, determined to attract no attention. The launch was waiting for her and, cradling Hoppy in her arms, she climbed straight in, loving the breeze cooling her as the craft raced across the waves to the giant matt-black yacht anchored out in the bay.

She had expected to have a moment to remove her unflattering outfit before she joined Jace but she was stymied when he greeted her as she stepped off the launch.

'What on earth are you wearing?'

Gigi dragged her dismayed gaze from his lean, powerful physique. As usual he looked the height of casual sophistication, black curls tousled, long thighs encased in fitted chinos, muscular chest covered in a T-shirt, and every time he breathed she could see his incredible pec and ab muscles expand and release. Her mouth ran dry. Only realising then that he was still awaiting her reply, she muttered, 'It was a disguise. I'll take it off now that I've arrived—'

His flaring ebony brows creased. 'Why would you wear a disguise?'

'Because photos were published in one of today's newspapers showing my face and us *kissing*,' she revealed in unmistakable disgust.

Jace was taken aback by her attitude because all the young women he knew relished such appearances in print with him. He crouched down to pet Hoppy, who bounced over to him on his three legs and then wandered over to Mo to get reacquainted, not one whit nervous of the huge dog towering over him.

'I don't want that kind of public exposure,' Gigi added. 'I like my quiet anonymous life.'

Jace frowned. 'I'm sorry. I can only control the publicity when I'm in private places. In my company there's always a risk of photos being stolen.'

'It's not your fault. Let me get changed first,' she said.

Jace's bright green gaze arrowed down into hers. *Thee mou*, she was beautiful, unadorned as she was, sunlight glimmering off her streaky brown and blonde hair. She was a picture: the slender column of her neck rising from the jumbo-sized hoodie, the big blue eyes, the naturally cushiony pink lips. His groin tightened and he concentrated on having her shown into a cabin. She emerged within two minutes, disconcerting him once again with her speed. There she was clad in simple shorts and a T-shirt worn over some kind of swimwear, for he could see the straps at the neckline, and anticipation almost made his mouth water. He began wondering for the first time if it was sexier when a woman showed less skin. Certainly, it was not a female habit in his vicinity. His pool parties on the yacht almost always featured at least one naked exhibitionist and once one person stripped, others invariably followed.

'So, what are your plans for the rest of the day?'

'Lunch at a little taverna on a small, quiet island and bathing or sunbathing or whatever. Relaxed. I assumed you would prefer that.' Jace hesitated. 'Alternatively we could go shopping somewhere—'

Her delicate nose wrinkled. 'Why would I want to go shopping? This is time off. I want to relax.'

Why would I want to go shopping?

Jace was amused by that innocent question but not at all surprised by it as he led her out onto the upper deck and ordered drinks.

Having released her hair from her ponytail, Gigi stood at the deck rail as the yacht sliced through the waves, her hair blowing back from her face. Jace slotted a moisture-beaded glass into her hand. 'We'll be getting off in little more than ten minutes,' he told her. 'You must've got a shock when you saw that newspaper. With hindsight, it was foolish for me to accompany you back to the harbour.'

'I didn't see the paper until my father and my brothers brought it to me. They were all furious,' she revealed tightly.

'Your father and your brothers?' Jace repeated. 'Are you saying that you have a family on Rhodes?'

'Calling them family would be stretching the truth. I only met them eighteen months ago. Before that, my Greek father and my half-brothers were total strangers—'

'You're half Greek,' Jace mused in surprise. 'How come you didn't already know them?'

Gigi winced. 'I'm afraid I *still* don't know my parents' story. My mother was very private, and she got exasperated when I asked awkward questions, calling their brief relationship "old history"—'

'It was *your* history.'

'Yes, I thought so too,' she agreed, folding her arms. 'I hoped my father would fill in the blanks but it's quite obvious that he doesn't want to. I suppose that's because he was married at the time with four young boys of his own. My mother was in Athens attending a conference and that's when they met. She did tell him about me.'

'Is it really that important to you now?'

'After my mother died suddenly from an aneurysm, I was looking for a family connection and Rhodes was the only place to look,' she confided with a shrug. 'So, I found a job on the island and then phoned my father—'

'And what was his reaction at that stage?' Jace pressed curiously.

'He seemed keen, he seemed pleased. Only he wasn't so enthusiastic once I was actually here.' Gigi sighed. 'He said I should move in with his mother, who had space…and I did, only to discover that what she really needed was a carer, so I became a convenient lodger there for the whole of my first year here. I loved Helene and got on very well with her though. Unfortunately, Helene didn't seem to know how her son and my mother got entangled or what the fallout was from it. My father obviously didn't confide in her at the time and she passed away about three months ago. I'm planning to return to the UK at some stage but I don't know when. I enjoy my work here and it's given me good experience but…'

Jace tensed at the news that she already had plans to leave Greece. 'Drink up…we're here.'

Gigi was pensive for a moment, acknowledging that she was not as keen to return to the UK as she had once been. Even working out the sheer expense of putting her pets into quarantine and the distress that that would cause them left her tummy churning. Furthermore, she had left no close friends behind, indeed had little to actually return for. At least, she recalled, until her mother's property in the UK finally sold and that last tie was cut. She drained her glass thirstily and stared up into the bright blue sky and then lower, to the rocky cliffs ringing a small unspoilt and empty beach. A haze of scrub and sturdy little trees growing out of the rock crevices clung to the steep gradient. 'Is it a big climb?'

'No, and you have appropriate footwear. There's a path.'

Clutching her bag and followed by the two dogs, Gigi climbed out of the launch onto the soft sand. Jace jumped down beside her, sunglasses anchored on his nose. She took notice of the four-man-strong security team that followed them. No, Jace was never alone except in beds and bathrooms, she reflected wryly. That had to be a drag for him but possibly he had grown up with similar protection and he had got so used it, he barely even noticed his silent backup any more.

He took her to the end of the path, a hand curved to her elbow as they began to follow the zigzagging path that slowly climbed upward. 'You've been here before,' she guessed.

'Many times, but this is the first time I've brought a guest. I come here when I'm in the mood for my own company. I hope you're comfortable with rustic surroundings. The food is amazing and the views are spectacular.'

He hauled her up the last few feet and steadied her as she studied the rock terrace built right on the edge of the cliff. 'Epic,' she pronounced, strolling up onto it to study the view of the glimmering sea in sunshine and the yacht far below them.

A little man came out and chattered up a storm about

what was on the day's menu. Evidently, there *was* no written menu. Gigi sat down in the shade at a home-made table, which their host proceeded to clean and polish. A younger man delivered glasses and a jug of chilled water. The dogs lay down in the shade, Hoppy edging closer and closer to Mo, who treated him like a puppy.

Jace recommended the fish and she went with his choice. She sat back in her surprisingly comfortable chair.

Jace levelled narrowed shrewd green eyes on her tranquil face. 'Why did your family bring that newspaper to you?'

Gigi winced. 'Don't ask—'

'I've got to ask,' he parried. 'I'm assuming it relates to me in some way—'

'According to them, no decent woman would date you—'

'You're the very first woman I've...er *dated*.' Jace seemed pained by the word, his lean, devastatingly beautiful face almost sombre.

'How is that possible with your reputation for loving and leaving women?'

'That's not dating, that's sex. I *don't* love them. I've never been in love and they know going in that I'll be leaving them eventually,' Jace replied drily, watching her expressive eyes as closely as a hawk in search of prey. 'I don't play guessing games with women. Everything is open and upfront—'

Gigi's brain was whirling round as fast as a merry-go-round, troubled by his honesty. 'So, what on earth are you doing with me?' she asked, smiling at the older man as he brought bread and cheeses and a bottle of wine to the table.

'I haven't worked that out yet,' Jace admitted with a compelling smile. 'When I have, I'll let you know. One glass?' He lifted the wine bottle.

'I'll have one.'

The bread was still warm from the oven and delicious with the salty cheese. The fish was fresh and tender and it melted in her mouth. It was a lazy meal and the conversation was good as well. Jace was astonished when she admitted that she was only twenty-three years old. He understood only after she admitted that she had always been on an accelerated programme of learning at school and had in fact graduated from university with her first science degree at the age of fifteen.

'So, nerd wasn't an exaggeration,' Jace quipped.

'No, not when it came to me. I was always with older students, which meant that my social life was a dead zone because I was out of step with my peers. It's only as I've got older that I've appreciated that it's not in my nature to be a social whizz kid.'

'You're sociable enough for me,' Jace murmured. 'I may have the reputation of a party animal, but I think that's the reverse side of the coin to working very long hours.'

They strolled back down the path to the beach, where a blanket had already been laid out with a drinks cooler.

His life was smoothed and polished by great wealth and the wheels were greased by his many staff. Gigi shed her shorts and her T-shirt and then felt suddenly, unusually self-conscious. There was nothing daring about her halter neck denim-blue bikini, little cleavage and very little of her derriere on show. In fact, she owned more revealing underwear than what she wore to swim. But for all that, somehow Jace was contriving to look at her as though she were stark naked and in possession of one of those spectacular cover-girl figures that always captured male attention. Turning pink, she walked into the water and within minutes she was swimming, fast and strong and confident, the way she had been taught, but her mind was utterly focused on Jace.

That wasn't like her. As a rule, she was only serious about work. Her profession was her life and it gave her confidence. Her job was a vocation and she loved the animals she worked to help. She had had to be strong to succeed so young in her chosen field and, in many ways, it had validated the choices her mother had censured her for making.

Jace, however, was showing her that she had more layers of mental and physical response than she had ever believed. He kissed her and the world fell away and that sounded like an adolescent's dream, but it had truly happened that way. For the first time she had wanted a man. And Jace might be the wrong man in terms of a future, but, in reality, did she want a serious future either? She was twenty-three years old and hers had been a relatively sheltered life in terms of the opposite sex. She was just finding her feet in the world. She didn't want to be tied down, married or someone's partner. Her job was her world. She loved it. So, sex with the right guy was finally on the table and justifiable. Why deny herself what she wanted when a guy as uninterested in commitment as she was magically appeared in front of her? Yes, he *was* magic, she reflected dizzily.

She was an excellent swimmer into the bargain, Jace noted without surprise. Mo was sitting just above the tide line, Hoppy beside him whining, both dogs anxiously awaiting her return. Jace was thoroughly abstracted after that view of Gigi in her faded old bikini that concealed far more than it revealed. But her shape was…divine. Perky little breasts, tiny waist, a bottom as shapely as a sun-warmed peach. He had wanted to put his hands on her so badly he had dug them into the sand to prevent himself from making the wrong move. Since when had he behaved that way? Self-denial didn't come naturally to Jace Diamandis, any more than being serious about a woman.

He didn't do that emotional stuff. And that was what she wanted. She might not have said so but he could read between the lines. But emotions would blunt his killer edge in business, soften him, *weaken* him. He had learned one hard lesson from his chequered childhood: *don't fall in love*. Argus Diamandis had fallen madly in love with Alessia Rossi, Jace's mother, the famous Italian opera singer, and he'd been jealous, possessive and *obsessional* about her. He might have remarried but even Evander, who had thoroughly disliked his eldest brother, had conceded that Argus had never recovered from Alessia's desertion or her death. And the aftermath of an obsessional love of that nature going wrong was often the very reverse of love, as Jace had learned as a child when he had been rejected by his father. Love like that was like a dangerous thread of instability in a man's character and the very idea of it creeped Jace out.

His grandfather's bête noire had been Electra Pappas, an heiress, who had put him through hell with her tantrums and flirtations. Yet even knowing her inclinations, his grandfather had married her, only for the marriage to crash into divorce within months. Ten years later, the couple had remarried, and Electra was now Jace's highly respected, widowed grandmother, soon to make her eightieth birthday. So, his grandfather had been obsessional too when it came to that *one* woman. A chill filtered down Jace's taut spinal cord. He wasn't about to follow in his predecessors' footsteps. He should be holding Gigi at a distance, looking for casual, replaceable, *easy*, not toeing the line for some woman who couldn't even be bothered buying a new bikini for his benefit!

At that moment, Gigi walked out of the water, casually wringing the salt water from her long hair with her hands. And Jace took one look at her, that shapely body streaming with water, that pouting pink mouth smiling, and he vaulted upright instantaneously. A siren singing on some rocky outcrop could not have yanked a stronger response from a sex-starved sailor, he conceded grimly.

'My goodness…you look very serious,' Gigi remarked, dropping down to her slender knees on the blanket and reaching for a towel.

Towering over her in swim shorts, even though he wasn't smiling, Jace looked drop-dead, lethally and heart-stoppingly gorgeous and sexy.

Jace gazed down into those cornflower-blue eyes and crouched down to her level. His big hands carefully framed her cheekbones and he leant forward slowly to kiss her.

'We can be seen by your security—' she gasped.

'Don't care.'

And he kissed her and it was everything, a sweet vein of sensual delight that tunnelled straight down to her feminine core. Her thighs strained together, seeking to quiet the burn of response. He tugged her to him with strong greedy hands and as she overbalanced down onto his lap she could not have missed registering how aroused he was. *Jace—*'

'I need to go into the water to cool down…or go back to the yacht.' It was the essential Jace, cool, straight, unapologetic. But there was nothing cool about the fire in the compelling emerald-green eyes trained on her for an answer.

'Yacht,' Gigi almost whispered, almost unnerved by her own daring.

Gigi glimpsed the flash of surprise he couldn't hide

and a deep flush scored her cheeks. Jace dug out his phone, spoke not quite levelly into it and then walked out into the water anyway, grinning back at her with sudden scorching appreciation.

CHAPTER FOUR

JACE WRAPPED HER in towels like an Egyptian mummy and swept her off her feet to carry her on to the launch when it arrived to collect them all.

'I must look ridiculous covered up like this!' She hissed the complaint in his ear as the launch approached the yacht. 'Put me down...'

'I'm preserving your privacy.' Jace was fiercely determined that he alone would be lusting after that glorious face and body of hers. The crew and his protection team were mostly male and men would be men: they would look, wonder, fantasise. Only, he had deprived them of that opportunity because in the present and, naturally, for a limited time, the only man who would be picturing Gigi naked would be *him*.

'Put me down, for goodness' sake!'

'The towels would fall off,' Jace overruled, manoeuvring the two of them safely off the launch and heading straight for the lift to hit a button with his elbow.

'I don't like domineering men—'

'Of course not,' Jace murmured levelly. 'Given the chance, you'd be doing the domineering.'

'That's not true,' Gigi insisted, one arm round his neck to keep herself steady while her nostrils flared on the wonderful smell of his skin. Salt water, fresh air, cedarwood laced with something that was just intrinsically him.

Ought she to tell him that he would be her first lover? Why should she care if he thought that was a bit strange? After all, with Jace Diamandis in the starring role, there was nothing surer than the reality that this would be a one-night stand. That was how the cookie crumbled. She needed to keep that in mind from the outset. Jace might be a playboy but at least he was an honest one. He hadn't fed her a single line or pretended to be something he was not. Somewhere deep down inside her she was conscious of a sharp little pang of regret that she would not see him again because she liked him, honestly *liked* him and that was why she had decided to go to bed with him. That tempting and rare combination of liking and dynamite chemistry might never come her way again, she reasoned.

Jace set her down in a huge room and she wouldn't have known she was on a yacht if she hadn't seen, beyond sliding glass doors, the stretch of a furnished deck terrace looking out to sea. She turned uncertainly, letting one of the towels swirled around her fall to the floor. Her attention fell on a simply vast bed and her mouth ran dry.

'Would you like a drink?'

Gigi spun round. 'Some water, please.'

'You're very tense,' Jace breathed, ebony brows pleating. 'Maybe you need more time to consider this—'

'I didn't expect to have to talk about it,' Gigi protested, gulping down her water as though she would never see water again, feeling the hot colour climbing below her skin and knowing there was nothing she could do about it.

Amusement lightened the tension on Jace's lean dark face. 'You assumed I would throw you on the bed like some caveman and get down to it without a word exchanged? Even I am not that crass.'

'You're embarrassing me. I haven't done this before,' Gigi admitted half under her breath. 'I wasn't going to mention it but you made me nervous.'

His brow creased, intense green eyes narrowing. 'Haven't done it before? Sex? That's not possible—'

Gigi lifted her head high, cornflower-blue eyes unflinching. 'It's possible because here I am.'

Troubled more than he wished to admit by her admission, Jace dragged in a slightly ragged breath. 'I haven't been with a virgin before, but I'll be very careful,' he murmured huskily. 'But stop right now if you're not sure. I definitely don't want to be the guy you regret.'

And even as he told her that, he wanted to laugh at himself. Since when had he cared that much about a woman's finer feelings? Yet he definitely knew that he didn't wish to be Gig's bad memory. And even as he then began to wish that he would *not* be her first lover, he knew it would be a lie. It was absolutely an honour that he wanted for himself. In some strictly temporary way she felt special and he felt a strong need to make everything special for her.

While Jace agonised over whatever he was agonising about, Gigi flopped down on the side of the bed and kicked off her shoes. 'I need a shower. I'm covered in salt.'

Emerging from his fugue, exasperated by his inability to concentrate, wondering if he could lay that rare affliction at the door of overwhelming sexual hunger and relieved by that explanation, Jace strode across the room and thrust open a door.

The washing facilities were to die for, sheer glass and black marble that shimmered with metallic golden streaks. Stripping off her wet bikini, she stepped into the shower, wishing she had thought to ask for her bag, although, frankly, it hadn't occurred to her that she might decide to stay the night with Jace, so her bag didn't contain so much as a toothbrush. But the shelving contained everything that a woman might want, she discovered, wrinkling her nose at the obvious thought that Jace regularly had women in his shower. What business was that of hers?

'There are no fairy-tale princes out there,' her mother had told her sharply when she was fourteen, ripping down a pin-up poster of a boyband member from her daughter's wall and scrunching it before tossing it in the bin. 'Get used to that idea now and you'll be the happier for it. Take your pleasure from men if you wish but don't expect anything else from them. They're only good for that one thing.'

Suppressing that unpleasant recollection of her mother's cynical distrust of the entire male sex, Gigi dried her hair and freshened up, unsurprised to find a still wrapped toothbrush in a drawer full of them. And she thought the half-brothers closest to her age were man whores? She shut her eyes tight, reminded herself that if she was using Jace, he was using her and that there was nothing wrong with that physical exchange. Even her cold-natured mother would have agreed that point. The same woman had insisted she went on the contraceptive pill at fourteen, saying that she didn't want any 'little mistakes'. Gigi had guessed right then that she had not been born the child of a planned pregnancy.

Even the effect of a cold-shower finish did nothing to lessen Jace's arousal. He was thoroughly fed up with his misbehaving body and the lack of adult control he was displaying. This was *not him* because he had never been desperate for a woman in his life.

A towel looped round her like a sarong, Gigi emerged from the bathroom, so nervous and awkward that her teeth were almost chattering together. The break between leaving the beach and arriving in Jace's bedroom had stretched too long for her relaxation to last.

Jace stretched back against the headboard, the sheet dropping to his waist, a vision of unashamed masculinity, revealing wide smooth brown shoulders and his muscular torso. He took in one glance of Gigi, blondish brown hair waving round her shoulders, blue eyes bluer than the sky, shapely curves safely covered in towelling, and he was off the bed faster than the speed of light without even thinking of moving. He scooped her up into his arms and then froze, struggling to think about what he was doing and why he was continually acting on some sort of subconscious inner voice that prompted him into weird behaviour around her.

Gigi let her head fall back against his arm, long silky hair brushing his thigh, blue eyes bright with laughter. 'I think I could get used to being carried around like a princess without your habit killing my domineering tendencies.'

'It takes one to know one,' Jace quipped.

And then just as she was thinking that she enjoyed his more sensitive side, which he had shown her when he earlier gave her the choice to step back from intimacy again, he kissed her. The whoosh of explosive hunger he could depth-charge through one kiss annihilated every logical thought. Her fingers crept up into his curly hair and held him to her, rejoicing in that shiny luxuriance and the smell of him that close. She felt as though every kiss she had had when she was younger had merely been a dress rehearsal for Jace and a complete waste of time. He dallied and he teased when he kissed, stroked her lips, nibbled a little, explored. It was so sensual, so sexy it should've been forbidden.

Slowly, gently, he began unwrapping the towel and sure fingers cupped the warm weight of a small breast, his thumb rubbing back and forth across the diamond-hard tip, sending little spears of desire hurtling through her. She quivered as he found the other, unexpected heat stabbing through her as the caress grew a little rougher and then he bent his head and took the throbbing peak into his mouth and sucked hard and pleasure engulfed her in a floodtide of response.

From that point on, it was a little like a dreamworld for Gigi because nothing happened as she had dimly expected it would. He shifted her down on to the bed and discarded the towel. He surveyed her as though she were a work of art and, later, she couldn't credit that she had lain there and simply let him look at her naked, but, in that moment, his rapt expression truly made her feel like the most beautiful woman in the world.

He came down to her, naked as she was but bronzed, muscular and beautiful, and suddenly she was as enthralled with him as he appeared to be with her. He kissed her again, skated a hand along one slender thigh while his mouth sought her breasts again and the surge of dampness she felt at the heart of her mortified her for a split second until she reminded herself that it was normal.

His fingers played between her thighs. He was very subtle, evidently gauging by her response what kind of touch she enjoyed. She appreciated how precise he was, the care he was giving to their encounter and she had no sooner thought that than she told him.

Jace lifted his tousled head to look down at her transfixed. 'Are you *rating* me?'

Gigi laughed. 'Well, you've got my vote—'

A smile chased the tension from his lean, dark face, lighting up his incandescent green eyes. 'You're very different from other women—'

'No, don't tell me that. I know I'm a bit off the wall. I don't need you to confirm it—'

'Even if I like it?' An ebony brow elevated.

'I shouldn't have interrupted you.' Gigi dealt him a teasingly pious glance and he laughed then.

As if they had all the time in the world, he worked his sensual path down her slender body and the little quivers of arousal began to build in strength. He settled his hands on the curve of her hips and lowered his head to the tender pink flesh between her thighs. She wasn't sure if she wanted something that intimate and then she reminded herself that essentially she was experimenting with Jace and exploring possibilities, so why not explore them *all*?

What she also wasn't expecting was how very fast his expertise drove her totally out of control. Hunger was a drumbeat in her pelvis that made her writhe and gasp and moan. Intense sensation gripped her in a steely hold and before she knew where she was she was reaching an unfamiliar plateau of pleasure that lit her up like a thousand fireworks inside and out.

'Are you on birth control?'

Gigi winced. 'No. Used to be, not any more—'

'Why did you stop?' Jace asked curiously, not notice-ably bothered by her negative response.

'My mother insisted I went on it at fourteen. I wasn't sexually active and I very much resented it. I stopped taking it about a year afterwards…it was my first rebel-lion against her expectations—'

'What was the next?' he could not resist asking.

'I suppose it has to be dropping out of medicine and choosing veterinary surgery instead. My mother wanted me to be a doctor but it wasn't for me. I'm better with animals than people,' she said quietly.

'I think you'd have been a winner with people as well if you'd had the right support to believe that,' Jace countered.

'My mother never forgave me for my change of heart. Once I reached eighteen, she stopped her financial sup-port, which of course was her right…hence my student loans, but I've never regretted the decision.'

'I wouldn't have met you if you hadn't been a vet.' Jace tensed, not liking that idea but so irritated by that awareness that he immediately tugged Gigi back into his arms. 'We're losing focus here—'

'Don't you talk in bed?'

'Never,' Jace admitted, his sensual mouth compress-ing before he nipped at the edge of her shoulder and kissed a deeply sensual path across it to her throat, where he dallied at her pulse points, smiling again into that kiss as he saw the pulse at her delicate collarbone go crazy and her pupils dilate again.

Once they got out of bed, he would give her dinner and let her leave, he bargained with himself. No, that could make her feel *used* and no way was he doing that to her!

He let his fingers slide into her hair, relishing that softness, that absence of product that left the strands flexible. He gazed down into her blue eyes and felt triumphant that he had her with him and hadn't allowed the less presentable flaws in his driven nature scare her off. He was thinking too much. He didn't know what had got into him. Performance anxiety? He didn't want to hurt her. That was what was wrong with him, he reasoned with relief. Female friends had told him that their first sexual experiences had been basement-level bad, and naturally he wanted something better for Gigi. Only a selfish bastard wouldn't be concerned on that score. When did I *stop* being a selfish bastard? he wondered.

Gigi ran exploring hands down over his torso, fingers delighting in the indentations and the hard muscle that was such a contrast from her own softer curves. Jace almost shuddered beneath her touch and returned to kissing her with hungry fervour. She arched up to him in response and was empowered by his hungry groan. He shifted against her and she felt him hard and ready at her core. Without hesitation, she lifted her legs and curved them round him, urging him on. After all, she didn't think it would be that much fun for her and she knew it would probably hurt. Anticipation was not her friend at that moment.

Jace braced his hands on the mattress to stare down at her with exasperated green eyes that scorched her like flames. 'We do this slowly or not at all,' he breathed.

'There's two of us here and I have a voice too.'

'Gigi—'

'If you expect me to stay in this bed another thirty seconds—'

Put to the test, Jace flexed his hips and surged into her like an invasion force. As he tilted her thighs back to gain depth, a sharp pang of pain shot through her lower body and she gasped. 'Oh, well, that's done, then,' she pronounced with satisfaction. 'I expect that's the worst over with.'

Jace gritted his teeth together. 'You're making me feel like a science experiment—'

He sort of...*was*, as Gigi saw it. She cringed at that insensitive inner recognition and closed her eyes tight lest he could read her expression.

'So,' he breathed, mastering his temper. 'Stop talking. I don't need egging on to the finish line like a child in his first race!'

'I'm sorry,' she whispered. 'I don't have conversational filters.'

He pulled out of her, watching her try not to wince, and then pushed into her again with decisive speed. And on the strength of that single movement, Gigi forgot what she had been talking about, forgot what she had been worrying about and experienced that first seductive taste of sensual pleasure. He was an incredibly tight fit inside her, stretching her inner sheath with an efficiency that was uniquely enthralling. Her mind went blank as that glowing warmth filtered through her and all of a sudden she was in the moment again and wanting more. Excitement sparked as his pace increased, providing her with intense sensation that made her heart race.

'Good?' Jace checked, embarrassed by the fact that for the first time in his life he was concerned.

'Don't you *dare* stop!' Gigi launched up at him, her hips rising to his in a language older than time.

Jace bestowed a dazzling smile down at her and thought of all the many, many things he still had to do with her. He shifted position, picked an angle, watched the flush of response rise up over her face, picked up pace again.

An electrifying tingle ran down Gigi's spine. Her entire body was thrilling to the surfeit of pleasure she had never known before. He drove into her harder and faster and tiny jolts of lightning tightened like bands round her pelvis. She struggled to keep a lid on her excitement and that drowning desire but as it built and built like an alarm clock ready to go off, she realised that she couldn't control it, couldn't stop it if she tried. When another climax engulfed her, she quivered and cried out, moaned, hearing herself, despising herself and, out of control, she was sent gasping and flailing into an explosion of pleasure that utterly consumed her.

Jace threaded a line of tiny kisses down over her drowsy face. 'Admit it...you liked it—'

'Don't talk,' she urged, her body too heavy, her brain too drained at what she had learned about herself for her to stand examination of any kind.

She dozed off without even being aware of it. Jace surveyed her in fascination. That was another thing that had never happened to him before: a woman just going to sleep as if he weren't there. As if he had indeed merely been an *experiment*? He suppressed that toxic suspicion. He was grateful that she was so different from the other women he had known. No flattery, no calculation, no apparent greed, no false front, no lies, the complete opposite of his cousin, Seraphina, who was as artificial and treacherous as Gigi was not. Gigi's qualities were solid gold in the Diamandis family where no woman he had met within the family circle saw him as anything other than a rich trophy to be caught. Not that he wanted her long term, of course he didn't! He was committed to his freedom from all such ties.

And while reassured by that conviction, Jace got on his phone and ordered a dinner for them that evening and wondered where she would like to go when he took her out. A nightclub? It didn't strike him as a very good fit for her and she had nothing to wear. He went into the bathroom to clean up and only then noticed that the contraceptive he had used had torn. He groaned out loud in consternation. As Evander's name swam onto his phone screen, he walked out onto the terrace naked to talk without disturbing Gigi.

'I thought I'd have heard from you by now,' his uncle said tautly.

'Why?' Jace raked his fingers through his tousled curls, cursing them the way he always did but his pride was too great to get rid of them. It was the one reminder of his mother that he had and if his father had rejected him for his stupid hair and the colour of his eyes, he had felt stronger not altering his appearance in any way.

Evander swore in Greek, which was a rare enough event for Jace to tense and frown.

'It's your grandmother's eightieth birthday tomorrow!' Evander shot back at him a touch accusingly. 'There's a huge party for you to preside over on Faros with the whole family present. I told you about it weeks ago—'

'I know. I forgot.' Jace frowned, plunged into darkness at the prospect of a Diamandis family reunion at what was now, following his father's passing, *his* main home on the island of Faros. 'However, I made all the catering arrangements at the time. I've even bought the painting you suggested for her.'

'Good enough,' Evander grunted, soothed by those admissions. 'So, what time will you be arriving?'

'I'll text you.' Jace glanced through the glass doors at the barely noticeable presence in his bed.

Someone shaking her shoulder wakened Gigi. She stretched languorously before she opened her eyes and then it all came back to her.

'Where are my clothes?' she asked the stewardess.

The young woman pointed at the transparent garment carrier hanging on the outside of a swanky built-in closet. Gigi blinked and focused on the barely visible blue dress. 'That's not mine,' she said.

Jace strode in like a sudden gust of wind, instantly filling the space with raw energy and expectations. The stewardess looked relieved by his arrival and departed.

'Is it all right if I go for a shower?' Gigi asked uncomfortably, striving not to look at him, striving not to be sucked in by his compelling dark attraction. He was casually dressed in linen shirt and chinos, but they had perfect tailoring and bore all the hallmarks of expensive design and sophistication. His black curls were windswept, his bright green eyes luminous with sheer energy, his stance one of command.

His expressive brows rose. 'Why would you ask me that? Of course it's all right.'

'Where are my clothes?' she asked again.

'I've organised clothes for you to wear. However, if you want your own—' Jace drew out his mobile and issued instructions in that cool, polite way of his in Greek that always warned her that he was making specific orders.

'I'm going home,' she told him, even more uneasily. 'I don't need anyone to organise clothes for me. I'm sorry I fell asleep. You should've wakened me ages ago. I know I shouldn't still be here. I'm not that out of touch.'

'I don't know what you're talking about,' Jace said truthfully, dark brows drawing together.

'A one-night stand, you're supposed to get up and get out, not linger like yesterday's news—'

'This wasn't a one-night stand,' Jace objected with unexpected rawness.

'But you don't *do* anything else!' Gigi carolled in exasperation at his refusal to say it like it was while leaving her to gabble on in clumsy discomfiture.

'There's an exception to every rule.' Jace was studying her in growing disbelief that she could actually be attempting to ditch him. 'I had no indication that you were likely to wake up with such an idea. How could I have? I warned you that I didn't want to be the guy you regretted—'

'It's not that,' Gigi cut in, her face pink with mortification because she wasn't inconsistent. She did not regret what had happened between them but she did feel unnerved about the intensity of what they had seemed to share and deemed it the wisest course to immediately call time on seeing him again.

'That's good because you're trapped on *Sea King* for the rest of the night,' Jace revealed quietly. 'We're at sea...'

'At...*sea*?' Gigi gasped incredulously. 'How can we possibly be *at sea*?'

Jace laughed, which was the proverbial last straw in the dazed mood she was in. 'Are you worried about your pets? Don't be. The bird, the tortoise and the cat are all on board as well and I packed for you.'

'Are you seriously trying to tell me that you've kidnapped me and my pets from Rhodes?' Gigi shrieked at him, grabbing up the discarded towel still lying on the floor and anchoring it below her armpits to slide out of the bed.

CHAPTER FIVE

JACE STUDIED GIGI with incredulity. As she stalked into
the bathroom like an angry miniature Amazon warrior,
he was momentarily stunned by her attitude.

What was the matter with her? It was the weekend.
He already knew that she had no other plans. He had
taken care of the pet problem and the clothes problem.
Other women valued his attention to detail, his generosity and his talent for organisation. Why didn't she?

He knocked on the bathroom door. It opened a mere
crack. 'Yes?' Gigi enquired glacially.

'I thought you'd be pleased,' he admitted after a stark
instant of hesitation, because in Gigi's company occasionally he felt vaguely as though he were dealing with
an alien. Her reactions were never what he expected, and
her concerns were even more startling. He had devoted
himself one hundred per cent to her entertainment. He
had never done that for a woman before. Why would
she then assume that he saw her as being only a one-
night stand? Surely he had been obvious enough that
she could read the writing on the wall?

'How did you get into my house?' she demanded.

Jace gritted his even white teeth. 'The keys were lying loose in your beach bag. I helped myself.'

Gigi rolled big blue eyes at him in disbelief. 'And you believed that doing that was all right? Sending strangers into my home?'

'I went with them. The cat was hard to catch. He wasn't for going anywhere. He hid under the sofa with the tortoise—'

'He is a *she* called Tilly,' she snapped. 'Are you saying that you personally went through my belongings?'

Jace compressed his lips. *What* belongings? he almost quipped. There had been a very large rucksack and a couple of drawers of casual clothes in a room as small and unadorned as a nun's cell. Even though that had been what he'd dimly expected from Gigi, he had still been taken aback by how little she owned and how very little she had personalised her surroundings.

'Yes. I didn't think you would like a crew member taking care of it.'

'Or...*you*!' Gigi stressed, slamming the door in his face, aghast at the idea that he might have rummaged through her underwear drawer or noticed that she hadn't made her bed up because the bedding was in the washing machine.

She showered. She fumed. She made up long ranting speeches inside her head. Where on earth did he think he was taking her? She marched back into the bedroom, scooped her obviously freshly laundered clothes off the foot of the bed and disappeared back into the bathroom to get dressed in her denim shorts again. There was no bra. She hadn't thought through that she would need one after she took her wet bikini off. What had he packed in her rucksack for her and where was it? The whole time, she thought anxiously about the way Jace made her feel. Feeling anything that powerful frightened her. Her mother hadn't shown her love and neither had her father. It only made sense to Gigi that she should always keep her emotions under control and never expect too much from people and situations. That was how she protected herself. Only with the animals she loved did she let her guard down.

Another knock sounded on the door. She wrenched it open. Jace handed her the dress in the garment bag.

Gigi simply set it aside because she had no intention of wearing it. 'You really don't take hints, do you?'

'Not when I don't want to hear them,' Jace conceded. 'I promise that I'll have you back at work on time on Monday morning. There won't be any problems—'

Gigi dealt him a fulminating scrutiny. 'You should turn the boat around and return me to Rhodes right now—'

'I can't do that. I'm taking you to my grandmother's birthday party tomorrow. It's her eightieth,' he informed her. 'If I turn back, I'll be late and, as I'm the host, that wouldn't be acceptable.'

Taken aback by that announcement, Gigi closed her hands into fists. 'Why the heck would you take *me* to a family party? You hardly know me!'

'I loathe Diamandis family gatherings but I believe it will be bearable if you are with me to lighten the atmosphere,' Jace declared with grim assurance.

'Why couldn't you just wake me up and *ask* me if I wanted to go?' Gigi demanded in annoyance.

'You had already told me that you were free this weekend. I assumed you would spend it with me.' Emerald-green eyes fringed by lashes stark black and lush as lace rested hungrily on her. 'Particularly after this afternoon.'

A faint pink lit her cheekbones and a tugging sensation clenched between her thighs. Even the memory of being with him was shockingly physical. So, he fought dirty in a fight. How was that news? He was clever, manipulative and devious and, if she was honest with herself, he fascinated her because he was so different from her. But the fleeting vulnerability in his beautiful clear eyes when he admitted that he hated family get-togethers and that her presence would help touched something soft and tender inside her, something that made her shiver, something that made her feel weak. And she refused to be weak or sympathetic towards anything other than a voiceless animal, which depended on her for care. Jace was too risky. Dangerous energy and volatility ran through him like a life force.

She had been fifty per cent certain that what they had shared was a once-only encounter. She refused to have expectations of him. But Jace was changing the game, suggesting possibilities that were disconcerting.

'OK...you win. I'll make a large donation to the animal shelter where you work,' Jace announced without warning.

Gigi blinked in surprise and looked daggers at him. 'Is that how you buy yourself out of trouble?'

'You're not being reasonable—'

'You're not being reasonable. Why should I be?' she demanded.

'We can work it out over dinner,' Jace told her with an irreverent grin. 'I'm starving.'

'I want to see my pets first,' she told him briskly.

Tilly was strolling along a deck and wound herself round Gigi's ankles with a purr before moving on to investigate Jace's. Hoppy was nestling in a tiny corner of Mo's giant basket in the main saloon while Mo reclined in front of the basket as though he were guarding the smaller dog. Snowy was in the saloon as well.

'You don't choose your pets on the strength of their appearance,' Jace remarked.

'Snowy is moulting, so don't be rude. He'll look much better in a few weeks. Most of my pets are the no-hopers from the shelter. Hoppy's a street dog and he's a mixed breed. Add in his disabilities and there was nobody interested in adopting him. Snowy's owner just wanted rid of him because he's not a very good talker. Where's Humphrey?'

Humphrey was munching in a sizeable cage in a cargo compartment.

'What do you deem a large donation?' Gigi could

not resist asking Jace as he guided her back to the upper deck.

He quoted a sum that left her bereft of breath. 'Think of all the good that money could do—'

A steward yanked out a dining chair for her and she sank down, unnerved as he shook out her napkin and placed it as well. She felt surrounded, inhibited by the presence of the crew. She lifted the wine glass that had already been filled. Jace hadn't needed the assistance of alcohol to get her into bed; she had done that all by herself, surrendering to that addictive chemistry, she reminded herself ruefully. She was trying not to think of what he had said. But cash would rebuild the outdated animal housing at the shelter. She could not deny that his money would do a lot of good and it infuriated her that he was making her think that way.

'I *am* thinking of the good,' she told him abruptly when they were finally left alone. 'But I don't like the fact that you're buying yourself out of trouble...or that you're trying to bribe me.'

'Squeaky-clean morals,' Jace groaned with a reproving appraisal. 'Doesn't it matter that it would improve the facilities for both you and the animals you tend?'

'Of course it matters. But I don't own or run the shelter and I don't know what the board of directors would do with such a big donation.'

'I could give it on the assurance that you must have a say in how it's spent because I know that you will put your patients first. I'm trying to say sorry, Gigi…but you don't make it easy.'

'Because if I make it easy it's like patting you on the back and encouraging you to do something like this again!' Gigi shot back at him, clean out of patience. 'And I will not be bought or bribed or blackmailed by your wealth! That's *wrong*, Jace. And you still haven't apologised.'

'I apologise.' Glittering green eyes held hers fast and her heart began to beat very, very fast, her mouth running dry because the power and intensity of his gaze burned her. 'But I *did* genuinely believe that you would freely agree to accompany me to the party. I also thought you'd be relieved that I'd considered the care of your pets and what you would wear.'

'Other women would be relieved, wouldn't they?'

'But I enjoy being with you because you're not the same as other women I've known,' he pointed out.

Gigi wrinkled her nose. 'But sometimes, like now, when I'm being awkward, you wish I *were* the same,' she guessed.

Jace laughed, a husky, sexy sound that brushed over her skin like the soft smooth brush of velvet. Goose bumps erupted on the skin of her arms, a warmth flowering at her feminine core.

'So, you'll come to the party.' Jace regrouped with that statement and disconcerted her afresh.

'Your presence will take the attention off me, at least a little,' he pronounced with satisfaction, draining his wine glass, a movement of his hand dismissing the steward who had moved forward from the far side of the room to refill it.

'I don't enjoy being the centre of attention. I'm a backroom girl.'

'No, to me you're something much more,' he contradicted. 'I want to show you off.'

Gigi tensed at the concept.

'I'm proud of you. Why wouldn't I be? You're an intelligent, independent and compassionate woman with a career you love.'

'Thank you. On the strength of your silver tongue, I agree to pretend to be plus one tomorrow,' Gigi conceded, smiling as she settled her cutlery down on the plate. 'I'll fake it until I make it—'

'Why should you have to pretend?' Jace demanded.

'Well, I'm not your girlfriend so of course I'll be pretending—'

Jace closed a lean brown hand squarely over hers. 'You *are* my lover. There is no need for you to fake anything.'

'I know next to nothing about you!'

'You know enough. My education? My birthday? My favourite colour?' Jace imparted those details. 'And what do those extraneous facts tell you about me? Precisely nothing.'

'Although if I were an astrologer, the birthday might be helpful,' she told him deadpan.

'Droll...'

The rest of the meal passed at speed. Gigi's anger had faded or Jace had charmed it away. He was great company, lighter in heart than her friends back in the UK. Of course, why wouldn't he be? Born rich, handsome and destined for success, he could have little in life to complain about, aside from a cruel, selfish father and, possibly, an equally egotistical mother, both of whom were now past history. Jace didn't need to worry about student loans or rent or saving up to buy a first home. In short, the world was pretty much his oyster.

'We'll have our coffee out on deck,' Jace decreed. 'We have something more serious to discuss.'

Frowning, Gigi glanced at him but there was nothing to be read in his lean, strong face. They sank down onto a wonderfully comfortable couch, a faint breeze lifting her hair and playing with the strands. She lifted her coffee and sipped, relaxing back into the upholstery. 'The something serious?' she prompted tautly.

'The condom ripped,' Jace spelt out grimly. 'I'd be less worried if you were on birth control.'

Shaken, Gigi set the cup and saucer down again with a slightly jarring crash. 'My word… I wasn't expecting *that*.'

'Neither was I. It hasn't happened to me before. I'm very careful.'

'I should have stayed on some form of contraception for my own protection. The trouble is, I wasn't counting on meeting you and I hadn't met anyone in so long that I decided that there wasn't any realistic need for it.'

She sighed, contemplating the risk of an accidental pregnancy with a sinking heart. 'I've always wanted children but not this way, because I was an unplanned baby and I think my mother found me a huge responsibility and resented me for getting in the way of her work.'

'But from what I understand your mother was alone. *You* won't be. If there's a pregnancy, we'll handle the situation *together*,' Jace insisted, closing a lean hand over hers in emphasis. 'In spite of the way I may strike you, I'm not even a little irresponsible—'

'Only occasionally guilty of kidnapping sleeping women and unsuspecting animals from Rhodes!' Gigi chipped in with a rueful giggle. 'I'm not going to worry about what you've told me until there's something to actually worry about.'

But Gigi did feel embarrassingly guilty because she had urged him on when, had he gone slowly as he had clearly intended, the contraception might have worked fine. Unfortunately, she had been in a hurry to move past the potentially painful part to hopefully the more pleasurable conclusion.

'Come here,' Jace urged, stretching out to remove her coffee cup from her hold and settle it back on the table. 'I need to kiss you right now.'

He tugged her closer and then lifted her bodily over him, so that her legs fell either side of his. And as she came down on him, she could not miss out on the reality that he was hard and ready, his perfectly tailored trousers unable to conceal his arousal. She assumed that he didn't think that there was much chance of her falling pregnant because their discussion had failed to distract him.

'We're in a public area, Jace. I won't risk an audience,' Gigi warned him.

Jace groaned in her ear, the warmth of his breath fanning her jaw. 'You drive me insane!'

'It's your own fault. You've got a cast of thousands on this boat as crew and they are *everywhere*—'

'I only want to kiss you.'

'So you say, but I'm not sure you can be trusted,' Gigi confided, shifting back off him again and kneeling beside him instead.

Jace bent his proud dark head and dropped a brief kiss on her parted lips and then he sprang upright and scooped her up into his arms before she could even guess what he was intending.

'Let me down!'

'We have to go to where we won't have an audience,' Jace decreed, laughing as she punched his shoulder with an exasperated fist.

'Jace!' she protested as he finally slid her down onto her own feet in his bedroom.

'I'm succumbing to an overpowering need to get you horizontal.' As he spoke, Jace undid the button at her waist and ran down the zip on her shorts and then he lifted her up into his arms again, his big hands gripping her hips, and he crushed her mouth under his with such a surge of burning hunger that answering heat roared through her like a bonfire.

As he dropped her down on the bed, Gigi kicked off her shorts and canvas shoes and reached for him.

'I want you too,' she murmured intently, an electrifying thrill thrumming along every nerve ending as their eyes collided. 'I don't know what you've done to me.'

Halfway out of his shirt, Jace paused and braced both hands on either side of her flushed face. 'I wanted you the minute I laid eyes on you with my dog in the street—'

'I didn't look at you until we were indoors—'

'And what did you think?'

It was amazing the rush she could get from one hungry, demanding glance of those scorching green eyes of his.

'I thought you were too good-looking to be real and now I like you best when I've messed you up a little,' she quipped, ruffling his soft silky hair until it was thoroughly untidy.

And when he slowly tasted her parted lips again with sensual expertise, she gave herself up to the pleasure of it. She felt happier than she had ever felt. She felt wanted, appreciated, *special* for the first time in her life. It was a crazy infatuation and she refused to agonise over it. It wouldn't last for ever. Such insane flights of fancy as put two such different people in a relationship never did last. But while it was current, she planned to make the most of it.

Tossing a handful of condoms on the nightstand, he curved a possessive hand to a small, pouting breast, his thumb rubbing across the prominent peak, watching her spine arch and lowering his mouth there to hungrily tease. Her hips rolled, that insane desire twisting inside her, no more easily ignored than a tornado. Her restive hands laced into his curls and then slid down to his wide shoulders, smoothing over his skin. He traced the heart of her where she was warm and wet and, oh, so willing to be touched. She rolled over onto her side and found his sensual lips for herself.

His tongue darted and dallied while his fingers played and toyed with her most delicate flesh, pushing her closer to the edge. The hunger she was struggling to control leapt higher and higher like a runaway flame. She felt almost frantic as he repositioned her writhing body and sank into her with potent strength. She climaxed instantly, unforgettably, and she was shocked. Fireworks shot up in multicoloured sparks behind her lowered eyelids while a whoosh of pure sensation seized her convulsing frame. She trembled and blinked rapidly in the aftermath, stunned by the power of the experience.

'Now let's see if you can do that again,' Jace murmured thickly, excited by the way she had lost control in his arms.

'Doubtful,' she mumbled shakily, barely able to think straight after that shattering flood of all-encompassing pleasure.

And the second time it was a slow, steady climb to

those same heights, the very last word in sensual pleasure. She was drowning in the emerald-green depths
of his eyes when he pushed her out of the comfort zone
into a much faster rhythm and her body reacted as if
it had been waiting all its life to experience that overwhelming excitement. Her heart thudded at an insane
rate, her body jolting, wild elation grabbing her as she
hit the heights again.

Afterwards, she was limp and on the path to sleepy
exhaustion.

'So...' Jace murmured huskily as he leant over her and
dropped a kiss on her damp brow, long fingers threading her hair back from her cheekbones in a slow, sure
movement. His green eyes glittered as though someone
had scattered stardust in them. 'You'll wear the dress I
got you for the party...'

Gigi heaved a sigh. 'I suppose, since I really don't
have anything else—'

'And wear the shoes—'

'I guess,' Gigi framed drowsily, snuggling into the
pillow.

'And there's some jewellery—'

Gigi surrendered the pillow in dismay. 'I don't own
any jewellery—'

'I have my mother's jewellery. I'd like you to wear a
couple of the diamond pieces.'

Gigi made a face. Her mother had had no time for
such frivolous items as jewellery and had left her nothing in that line. When she was barely welcome in her

own family, the idea of wearing *his* family jewellery made her feel horribly uncomfortable. 'No, thank you. I'm not showing off family jewellery when I don't belong to the family,' she told him tartly. 'That would make me look like a *very* ambitious companion as well as being one who lacks good taste.'

'It's mine to do with as I wish. It would only be on loan for the day—'

'Doesn't matter. I don't want to borrow anything,' Gigi said squarely.

'You can think about it—'

'I've already thought and the answer is no, Jace. *No!*' she slung back at him with furious stress, snatching up her shorts, climbing into them by the side of the bed and grabbing her T-shirt to pull it on as well.

'It was only a suggestion. There's no need to lose your temper,' Jace breathed tautly.

CHAPTER SIX

'ISN'T THERE?' Gigi spun back to look at Jace, still busy tugging her hair out from below the T-shirt, an arc of colour now enhancing her cheekbones. 'If you don't get the answer you want, you *persist*. You can't deal with a negative answer when you want agreement. It makes me wonder what you're doing with me,' she admitted frankly. 'I'm not a dress-up doll, Jace. I'm not a yes-girl either. I am who I am and proud of it. I'm not going to a party to pretend to be someone I'm not because you would prefer a glitzier version of me than you actually have!'

'That's not what I said. I am happy with you as you are—'

'No, you'd prefer an improved edition and sorry, but you're stuck with me!' she countered angrily.

'Where are you going?' Jace demanded as she reached for the door handle.

'To find another bed. One that's empty. Did you pack *any* of *my* things?' she asked flatly.

Jace indicated a door. 'In the dressing room.'

Gigi stalked into the dressing room and opened

doors. Locating her rucksack, which had already been unpacked, she filled it again.

Wearing only a pair of black boxers, Jace lodged in the doorway. 'I don't want you to leave—'

Gigi gritted her teeth. 'You make me madder than anyone I've ever met!'

'Your temper is almost as bad as mine, just slower to rise,' Jace commented. 'Stay with me. I shouldn't have put on the pressure. I should've quit while I was ahead—'

Gigi groaned. 'It's too late at night for all this drama—'

'Drama was something I didn't do until I met you,' Jace admitted and a sudden sizzling smile lightened his expressive mouth while he carefully reminded himself that Gigi was only a temporary presence in his life. 'Lesson one, in a relationship listen to the other party. Lesson two, don't assume orgasms grant you a get-out-of-jail-free card. Lesson three, don't rile Gigi after midnight or she turns into a gremlin.'

An involuntary laugh escaped Gigi. She tapped a forefinger on his bare chest. 'No diamonds. We will get by fine without diamonds.'

Jace had already decided to get on his phone and find something that would be more acceptable to her than jewels, something that would make her smile, as she was smiling right now at him and it felt like liquid sunshine warming his skin. 'I'll have to make some calls early tomorrow—'

'It's already today and I haven't got a gift for your grandmother. I need a card, maybe some flowers—'

'I'll organise it.'

Gigi breathed in slow and deep and smiled again. What did he do to her? One minute she was raging and the next she was laughing. He had great charm when he wished to utilise it. Why did she feel as if she had known Jace for years? Where had the normal stranger barriers gone? She stuffed her rucksack back in the dressing room and undressed again to go for a shower.

The next morning, Gigi pulled on cool cotton trousers and a T-shirt. She wouldn't risk putting on the fancy blue dress until it was time to leave for the party. She was relieved that she hadn't worn it the night before.

Every tiny movement tugged on muscles somewhere inside her body and once or twice she winced and frowned, reminded more than she liked about the long, bold, brazen night that she had spent with Jace. Jace was like a wicked genie freed from a bottle. Every time he touched her, it was as though he bespelled her. A kiss, a fleeting caress and she was his again. She had never dreamt that she could want any man the way he made her want him and she didn't like that lack of control, that lack of true choice. It was as though her free will had been stolen from her. She had assumed that that intense sexual hunger would fade once satisfied but what did it mean when that didn't happen?

It was unsettling. Jace was supposed to be a fling, an

experience, an affair and nothing more, wasn't he? She didn't want to get hurt, she didn't want things between them to turn messy, no, once the party was over, she wanted her life back the way it had been.

But how could she *truly* say that she wanted that? If she was honest, she had got lonely, living her independent life while stuck in her safe routine. Jace had splashed colour into her world, brought her alive and only now was she recognising just how much she had stubbornly denied herself.

'Breakfast is waiting,' Jace called through the sliding doors that opened onto the terrace.

Breathing in deep, Gigi braced herself. Jace had already been up and about before she roused and when she had stirred in that empty bed the first thing she had looked for was *him*. That had scared her, for a long time ago she had learned the hard way not to let anyone get that close to her. Sooner or later, favourite nannies, teachers or housekeepers always moved on somewhere else, often without even saying goodbye. In the same way, her mother had died without ever trying to repair their fractured relationship and Gigi had lost any prospect of forgiveness and acceptance as well. She couldn't afford to get attached to Jace. He was a free and easy playboy with a notorious reputation, and she was just one more in a long line of women.

It didn't matter that he had got up in the middle of the night to let Mo and Hoppy in when Mo whined outside the door. It didn't matter that he had hugged her most of the night like a precious teddy bear. She was neither a dog nor a toy and she wasn't here to stay either. No, she was only passing through his life.

Jace watched Gigi walking out to the table, small and slim and graceful. And yet that perfect skin of hers glowed, her blue eyes sparkled, and her luscious pink mouth smiled. She was beautiful even though she didn't know it and she was *his*. That thought thundered back through him again and his teeth gritted. She was his… *for now*. He wasn't a one-woman man. Soon enough he would tire of her and then it would be over. The dogs swirled round her legs like a moving carpet of fur, begging for her attention.

'That's the island of Faros on the horizon,' he told her, deliberately directing his thoughts away from her.

'Our destination?' Gigi queried, fighting to drag her gaze from his tall, dark frame, but that was a struggle when she didn't want to look anywhere else or when he had been out of her sight for a few hours and she literally felt starved of seeing him.

'Yes. It's a private island.' She studied him intently as he spoke. His dark suit fitted him with exquisite, tailored perfection blended with designer style. With his glossy black curls and potent emerald-green eyes, he was electrifyingly sexy. Broad of shoulder, narrow hips, tight waist and long, powerful legs. And below the suit, he was all lean, hard muscle.

'Your family own it?' All of a sudden, Gigi was finding it very hard to breathe.

'I do.' Jace shrugged, watching her frown down at the bewildering number of choices on the breakfast table before helping herself to a simple cup of tea. 'The island has the only house in the family that's large enough to entertain the whole Diamandis clan. It usually belongs to the head of the family but because my grandmother didn't get on with her son Argus—my father—my grandfather left the house jointly to my grandmother *and* me... Argus was hopping mad.'

'Why didn't your grandmother get on with her son? He was her eldest child and often the eldest is the favourite—'

'She couldn't forgive him for rejecting me and when he tried to disinherit me, it was the last straw. They had a massive fight and I think they both said things that the other couldn't forgive.' Jace shrugged a broad shoulder ruefully. 'Argus loathed the fact that he couldn't use the big house on Faros. He felt it lowered his standing in the family. Status, appearances, reputation? They meant more than anything else to my father. He built a mansion of his own at the other end of the island.'

'Was he a good dad before your mother left him?' Gigi asked curiously.

'I hardly knew him...*or* her, if I'm honest,' Jace admitted with rueful regret, even while he wondered why he was confiding that truth to her when that admission had never crossed his lips before. 'That was the nannies and boarding school phase of my life. Both my parents were very busy people. Evander and Marcus changed

all that. Their care was much more personalised, much
more hands-on and day to day. They took me to school.
They attended prize days and Christmas concerts—'

Gigi was impressed by his sheer honesty and happy
that he was sharing such personal facts with her.
'They're the uncles that raised you?'

Jace nodded confirmation, watching her select a yogurt, the plainest on offer.

Gigi dipped the spoon and licked it, savouring the
creaminess, soft pink lips pouting for a split second.
Jace felt the throbbing pulse at his groin start up again
and he gritted his teeth. Gigi had been in his bed all
night and he had taken full advantage of the fact. Why
the hell was he still craving her like some wildly addictive drug? He glowered broodingly out to sea, his sensual mouth compressed over the lowering reality of her
overwhelming appeal for him.

Gigi finished the yogurt and slid upright again. 'I
need to hurry so that I can get dressed. You had better
hope that that fancy frock fits.'

'It should do.' His ebony brows drew together as he
swung back to face her, recalling a necessity he could
not afford to overlook. 'I'll organise a blood test for you
towards the end of next week and text you the arrangements. It will tell us whether you're pregnant days before an ordinary test would.'

Gigi glanced back over her shoulder in surprise. 'I
didn't realise that you were that concerned about that.'

'Obviously it's a possibility that we shouldn't ignore. I'll be away on business next week,' he warned her.

'It'll give us a break…after we've spent the whole weekend together,' Gigi pointed out quietly, feeling that she needed that time away from him to plant her feet firmly back on solid ground again.

The dress fitted like a dream. It was blue, neither too short nor revealing and it suited her better than anything she had ever owned. She eased her feet into the high-heeled sandals with their opulent pearl trim. Her legs looked unusually long even to her own critical gaze. She sat down at the dresser and braided her hair to put it up.

'I need make-up,' she told him wryly.

'I didn't see any in your house, didn't think of that,' Jace admitted. 'But there's a beauty salon onboard.'

Gigi was reckoning that her few bits of make-up were probably still in her bag under one of her coats in the hallway. She turned wide-eyed to stare. *Really?*

'And one of those beauty consultants.'

'Take me there,' she pressed without hesitation, knowing that a little primping was necessary for a high-society party.

He escorted her down to a lower deck and left her there with the chattering consultant. Thirty minutes later, she emerged again, convinced that she could hold her own in any gathering. Her enhancement was subtle and much better done than she could have contrived on her own. She looked natural and that was exactly what she had wanted.

Jace watched her step onto the launch and smiled. She looked amazingly beautiful in that dress, shapely legs on show but nothing else. She looked like a lady, elegant and collected. The neckline looked a little bare though, her slender neck unadorned. He still wished she had been willing to wear the diamonds.

The island was very green with trees and gorgeous in the sunshine. She glanced back at the launch leaving the small harbour again, white water eddying in its wake against the deep blue of the sea. A huge SUV whisked them through the bustling village, past the big Greek Orthodox church and uphill on a rough road. Within minutes they were turning up a paved lane bounded by palm trees.

'Does your grandmother live here?' Gigi asked.

'During the summer but once winter kicks in, she returns to the mainland.'

It was a very grandiose, palatial house stretching across the whole top of the hill. White walls, tall gleaming windows and elegant terraces overlooked the gardens and the bay below. 'Very impressive,' she muttered nervously.

The huge hallway was a rush of surging and busy people. 'Caterers,' Jace explained as an older man approached them, apologising in Greek for the disturbance.

Jace introduced her to Dmitri, who was in charge of the household, and asked how his grandmother was. He referred to her as 'Yaya', just as Gigi's family had labelled her late grandmother.

Dmitri grinned. 'Full of life today. Mrs Diamandis enjoyed her breakfast outdoors and even walked out to see her birds.'

'She likes birds?' Gigi queried in surprise.

'I've already told her about Snowy. She wants to see him. If he won a home in her fancy aviary complex, he would be fortunate indeed.'

His hand in hers, Jace strode ahead of Dmitri and led the way into an opulent sitting room that opened out into a shaded conservatory lush with tropical plants. 'Just in time for the festivities,' a lively voice announced.

And there in a basketwork armchair sat a little old lady with silvery hair and a delighted smile spreading across her soft, weathered face. 'Evander said you'd be late.'

'And yet, here I am in good time for lunch. This is Giselle Campbell… I call her Gigi. Gigi, this is Electra Diamandis.'

A hand was extended to Gigi as she was looked over from head to toe, but the smile remained, from which Gigi deduced that she at least looked acceptable. 'Happy birthday, Kyria Diamandis.'

She was offered a powdered cheek to kiss. 'Congratulations, Jace. You have finally brought a young woman home to meet me. Call me Yaya, Gigi, because you're obviously going to be family. Sit down and tell me all about yourself. My goodness, Evander and Marcus are in for a surprise!'

Lashes fluttering at that extraordinary welcome speech, Gigi wondered what was going on and she sank uncertainly down into the indicated seat.

'Jace always swore that the only woman he would ever bring home would be his intended bride.' Gigi's bare hand was lifted by her hostess. 'Taking your time about putting a ring on that finger, aren't you?' she shot at Jace with a warning look of concern.

Feverish colour lined Jace's high cheekbones as shock rocked him where he stood. He spread a troubled glance between the two women.

'Go and see your uncles,' Electra instructed. 'And by the way, I changed your catering arrangements for lunch. We're having a buffet instead of a sit-down meal. There's too many guests for the dining room.'

Looking a shade shell-shocked by the encounter, Jace studied Gigi's burning face and winced inwardly. He supposed he should have immediately contradicted his grandmother concerning Gigi's status in his life, but he had been too disconcerted by the reminder that he *had* once said that the only woman he would bring home would be his future wife. In addition, the old lady looked so happy with that interpretation that he had not the heart to disabuse her of the assumption. How many times had his grandmother bemoaned the fact that she was not yet a *great*-grandmother like her friends? Although it would be an even bigger shock for him if he turned out to be the *father* of that much desired great-grandchild, he acknowledged grimly.

'Jace told me you have a cockatoo who's looking for a home.'

'I didn't know that Jace had told you about Snowy—'

'Jace phones me every day,' Electra Diamandis revealed. 'There's not much he doesn't tell me.'

Gigi gripped her hands together nervously at that news and decided to keep the chat centred on Snowy as she advanced details on the bird.

'I have to apologise to you now in advance,' the old lady murmured very quietly. 'I didn't know until this week that Jace was bringing you and he hadn't invited many young people. I didn't want my party to be only the older folk and I invited a bevy of youthful beauties from the family to liven the men up.'

'Sounds exciting.' Gigi smiled and swept up the cold drink Dmitri brought her. She talked about her job and her pets while wondering why Jace's grandmother was so keen to see him married off. His reputation? Or did she just think it was time that Jace settled down? Why hadn't Jace put his grandmother right? Gigi felt as though she was being welcomed on a false premise and it embarrassed her. She was merely a girlfriend for the sake of appearances, not a future Diamandis bride.

Jace reappeared to collect her, allowing other family members to move in and sit down with Electra. He whisked her off.

'Why didn't you tell her that I'm not in line to become your wife?' she hissed at him.

'I didn't know what to say. I did say a long time ago that the only woman I would introduce to the family would be my bride, but I'd totally forgotten saying it,' he confided. 'It's just wishful thinking on Yaya's part and harmless conjecture.'

He took her straight to a pair of attractive older men talking in a quiet corner of the crowded hall. 'Evander... and Marcus. This is Gigi.'

'Evander Diamandis.' The tall man with the pepper and salt hair and beard gave her a firm handshake.

'Marcus.' Blond and British with wings of white over his ears and slighter in build than his partner, Marcus grinned at her. 'We've been waiting a very long time for Jace to bring home a girlfriend—'

'But we'll hold off on fetching my mother's engagement ring to give you,' Evander continued with wry amusement. 'I don't think you're quite ready for that as yet, but I'm afraid the rumours are flying round here already. Let my mother enjoy her eightieth, Jace, and dream her dreams undisturbed.'

'I intend to but thanks for not producing the ring on demand,' Jace murmured with a pained roll of his eyes.

'You can push off now and give us five minutes to get to know Gigi,' Marcus told him with amusement.

Jace had landed lucky with his second set of parents, she decided. Evander and Marcus were lively, entertaining company but Gigi was on edge, very much aware that she was being sized up.

'So, you're both still in the besotted phase,' Evander commented, startling her.

Taken aback by the observation, Gigi stammered, 'Er...no, I—'

'You can't stop looking for him and he can barely take his eyes off you for ten seconds,' Evander sliced in calmly. 'Not our business, I know, but it's good to see that he's opening himself up to more challenging possibilities.'

Jace reclaimed her as though he were snatching her from the jaws of death and she laughed with genuine amusement. 'They were very pleasant. Apparently, we're in the besotted phase.'

'Is that why I keep wanting to rip your clothes off?' His dazzling smile lifted the tension from his lean, dark face. 'Bless them, they do love to watch people. Let me show you around the house in case we get separated later.'

As they strolled around, she met more and more guests, including Jace's half-brother, Domenico, aka Nic, arm in arm with a very beautiful blonde. She found herself staring up at Nic, trying to see how much he looked like Jace, but the resemblance was only fleeting in his smile and other expressions.

The buffet would begin only when Electra Diamandis made her official appearance.

'You didn't tell me you had a brother,' she censured as he led her upstairs.

'I don't know him very well yet. My father remarried and he's the result. I first met him at our father's funeral. He's very successful in business and looks set to marry early. Perhaps he will make Yaya's dreams come true with a great-grandchild.'

'I hope we don't get faced with that issue,' she muttered unhappily.

'Never tackle trouble before it comes unless, of course, you can influence the outcome…and you *can't*,' Jace pointed out in challenge, pushing open a door on a wide airy room that seemed, by the number of doors visible, to yield entry to several other rooms. 'We are sleeping here tonight in the master suite. Your luggage will be brought here later.'

Trouble? Was that how Jace saw the risk of a pregnancy? Well, how else did she expect him to view it? Did she feel any different? At this stage of her life and career? For a split second, she had an image of a child who looked remarkably like a miniaturised version of Jace and, involuntarily, her heart lifted and warmed. If there *was* a child, she would raise her child with all the love and warmth her mother had denied her. She would make space in her busy life, she would make changes for her child's sake and put her child first. It didn't really matter how Jace felt about the prospect. She didn't need *him* to raise a child, she told herself fiercely, her natural independent streak taking charge of her.

'You've gone all serious now. I shouldn't have brought up *that* subject.' Jace sighed.

'*Are* we besotted with each other?' Gigi suddenly asked in dismay. 'I don't want to feel like that. I don't want you to be that important to me—'

Jace grinned down at her, slow and assured. 'I feel the same, but it doesn't seem to be something we have much control over.'

And without warning, long fingers traced her delicate jawline and curled round the back of her neck and he kissed her with all the hunger that had built since early morning and, if anything, her response engulfed his. They made it down onto the bed, kicking off shoes, and she shouted when he wrenched at her dress. 'Don't you dare rip it! I have nothing else to wear!' she warned him.

Jace ran down her zip and unhooked the neckline at a very decorous pace. He lifted it off over her head.

'We shouldn't be doing this,' she sighed without much fight in her.

Jace released her bra with a skilled hand. 'I guess this is what besotted people do,' he breathed thickly.

The burning heat and hunger of his kiss overwhelmed her. She couldn't resist him when that ache clenched between her legs. It turned her into a total hussy, who flattened him to the bed and ripped off his tie.

Jace sat up, his dazzling smile never more evident as he casually, gracefully undressed, skimming off everything until he was reclining beside her unashamedly naked and bronzed. 'I'm all yours.'

And she thought then, *If only he were*, and just as quickly she caught up on that reflection and drove it out of her head again. She wasn't going to fall in love with him. She already felt more for Jace than she was comfortable with feeling. Whatever he felt for her was sexual, nothing deeper, nothing lasting. She would be a very foolish woman if she dared to think otherwise.

Passion glittered in Jace's spectacular eyes and she quivered with helpless anticipation, her body even more wound up than her brain. She almost passed out with pleasure when, having protected them both, he sank lethally deep and sure into her and then there was the long climb to satisfaction followed by a frantic rush to get dressed and presentable again. There was a flush on her cheeks and a ripeness to the pouting pink of her swollen mouth that set Jace on fire again before he even got back downstairs. If this was 'besotted' it was joyful fun and excitement, he reasoned, and he could happily live with it.

When they entered the big room where the buffet was being served and where the guests were spilling out onto the outdoor terraces, Gigi became aware of just how much she and Jace were under close scrutiny, particularly by the young and beautiful women sprinkled through the crush.

'I think Yaya's fondest hopes have spread,' Jace opined. 'It should keep everyone polite and distant.'

'Why wouldn't they be polite?'

'My female cousins always assumed that one of them would marry me, so you're treading on toes, which is good.'

'How…good?' Gigi asked thinly.

'Well, if you're assumed to be my future wife, few will wish to get on the wrong side of you.' Jace laughed. 'And they're probably too busy gossiping to spare the time.'

'I don't like anyone thinking that I'm your bride-to-be,' Gigi admitted tightly.

'I apologise,' Jace declared, a touch brusque in his delivery, his dazzling eyes narrowing. 'This is my fault because I was reluctant to contradict my grandmother and disappoint her.'

'Don't worry about it. When they never see me again, they'll know the truth.'

Jace's lean, darkly handsome features were now taut, his sensual mouth compressed at the prospect of never seeing her again. 'Obviously.'

There was a sharp little silence and it occurred to her that she had been tactless being so blunt, and her face flushed. Suddenly she was mortified at her lack of generosity. What did it matter if a pack of people she would never see again believed she was something she was not? And furthermore, when Jace inevitably moved on to other women, the rumours would be exposed as trivial nonsense.

They sat outside on a shaded terrace, soon joined by Jace's brother and the blonde beauty, who was apparently, in spite of appearances, *not* his girlfriend but actually his best friend. She noticed that Jace was very quiet, and her healthy appetite died long before she went indoors to the cloakroom.

As she crossed the hall again, a tall, curvaceous blonde greeted her. 'I'm Seraphina Diamandis,' she said, much as if she expected Gigi to already know who she was.

'Oh?' Gigi remarked awkwardly.

'Jace was mine first. I thought you should know,' she announced with a subdued melodrama that widened her eyes and made her sultry lips pout.

'It's not really something that I want to talk about,' Gigi said gently, keen to avoid any kind of confrontation.

'I'm Jace's cousin.'

It put new light on keeping it within the family, Gigi conceded.

'I'll be at every family gathering you attend,' Seraphina informed her ominously.

'I don't care who was with Jace first,' Gigi confided. 'I only aspire to be his last.'

After that uneasy meeting, Gigi caught her breath again while photos were taken of them all. A sea of camera phones flashed as Electra opened a handful of presents, one of which was Jace's, a superb modern painting. His grandmother insisted on showing Gigi her art collection with Evander and Marcus in tow. She had no idea where Jace had gone but she learned a lot that she didn't know about art in such knowledgeable company.

Snowy the cockatoo had arrived from the yacht and

Electra accompanied Gigi out to see her aviary. The old lady had decided that she wanted Humphrey, the lazy, non-foraging tortoise, for her garden as well. Gigi had good reason to be grateful that she hadn't brought either Hoppy or Tilly out from the yacht, lest she find them being rehomed as well. She no longer needed to wonder where Jace had acquired his love of animals.

As Electra retired for the night, a DJ took over. Jace was drinking with a crowd of his male relatives and evidently not looking for her.

'Did you two have an argument?' Marcus asked while he put on a lively display of dad-dancing.

'A misunderstanding,' Gigi replied uncomfortably.

After a couple of hours socialising with Evander and Marcus, Gigi went over to Jace and told him that she was tired.

'I'll be up later,' he told her smoothly, catching her hand in his, lifting it towards his mouth and then letting it go again as if he didn't know quite why he had reached for it in the first place.

Gigi went up to bed, leaving Seraphina and her best friends doing some very suggestive dancing at the edge of the floor closest to Jace. So, she had put her feet in it with him, she told herself as she climbed into the comfy bed alone. She had acted insulted over being viewed as Jace's future wife and she had offended him. Why?

Her eyes stung. Perhaps her messy emotions were something to do with the fact that at that moment she had, crazily, wished it were truth and not mere rumour.

And she was ashamed of that weak spot inside her that wanted a happy ending against all the odds. She swallowed hard and lay awake for a long time waiting for Jace to join her, but she was fast asleep when he finally did in the early hours of the morning.

CHAPTER SEVEN

GIGI WAS WAKENED early by her phone the next morning and she found herself alone in the bed, only a dented pillow beside hers letting her know that, at some stage, Jace had shared the room with her.

Sitting up, flustered and still half asleep, she came instantly wide awake when she recognised the voice of the CEO of the animal shelter, her boss, Thea. She learned that there was such a crowd of paparazzi camped out waiting for her arrival at work that Thea thought it would be best if Gigi took some time off on leave and they brought in a locum. Although the police had moved the crowd out onto the pavement, the staff and the usual visitors were being harassed for information about Gigi.

Gigi spluttered out a surge of embarrassed apologies only to fall silent when Thea congratulated her on her engagement. Her…*engagement*? Deeming it wisest not to tell the truth in such circumstances, Gigi thanked the older woman and came off the phone again. Getting dressed in her usual casual shorts and a top, she went downstairs in search of Jace.

Dmitri showed her into the grand dining room where

Jace was chatting on the phone. He ended the call and turned to her, sheathed in fitted chinos and a casual jacket, a silk scarf at his throat, a warmer jacket tossed over a nearby chair. He looked effortlessly, sleekly European and as perfectly groomed as though he had walked off a modelling shoot. Her heart gave a stirring thud and stuttered inside her. She felt far too plain to be even seen in his sophisticated company.

'You must have risen very early,' she remarked, resisting the temptation to ask him what time he had come to bed. After all, he didn't owe her any explanations. Nor had his late night etched so much as a shadow on his lean, darkly handsome face.

Jace smiled as he sat down at the table. 'I'm always up at first light.'

'Someone's released photos of us at the party and announced that we're engaged to the media,' Gigi told him anxiously as she sank down into a seat beside him.

'One of the party guests with a phone,' Jace guessed grimly. 'We'll ride it out.'

'It's not so easy for me.' Gigi explained that she had been asked to take leave to minimise the harassment at the animal shelter.

'This is my fault. I'm sorry,' Jace said flatly, his exasperation making her feel mortifyingly raw. 'If I had stopped that rumour in its tracks, this wouldn't have happened. You can't even go home—'

Gigi frowned. 'Of course I can.'

'The paps will soon have your address as well. Stay onboard the yacht while I'm away,' Jace advised.

A lump formed in her throat and her eyes prickled and she looked away from him. 'I think we both need space right now and living on your yacht will only add substance to those rumours.'

Jace froze. For a split second, all he wanted to do was put a ring on her finger and tough the immediate future out, but that sudden surge of possessiveness and that desire for permanency appalled him, particularly when it pertained to a woman who had firmly rejected the concept of being his fiancée or his wife. Jace could never handle rejection easily because he came from a background full of similar rebuffs.

'That's a decision that only you can make,' he pointed out. 'But I don't agree with it.'

Colour flared in her cheeks again. 'How long will you be away?'

'About a week. You *could* come with me,' Jace murmured, startling himself with that impulsive invitation.

Gigi stiffened. 'Thank you, but no. But I'm sorry I offended you yesterday. I sort of felt trapped into a role I didn't feel comfortable in, and I took it out on you. I'm not very good at faking stuff…or lying.'

Long brown fingers closed over hers where her hands were knotted on her lap and her blue eyes flared up into compelling green framed with lush black lashes. 'I didn't think the situation through from your point of view—'

He leant closer, a lean hand reaching out to smooth

up her slender neck and ease her closer. His wide sensual mouth drifted slowly across hers and her heart hammered like crazy. He kissed her slow and he kissed her deep: it was not a casual caress. She wanted to grab him, hold him close, say stuff that she knew she shouldn't say to him, and those impulses scared her. She needed to get back in control of herself fast.

'Guess who's kicking himself now for not coming to bed sooner last night,' Jace growled. 'Our last few hours together and I chose to waste the opportunity—'

'It doesn't matter.'

Jace groaned. 'Even if you decide not to stay on the yacht while I'm away, leave Hoppy and Tilly onboard because if the paps stage a vigil at your place, it'll upset them.'

'Hopefully, this will all settle down in a couple of days,' Gigi said brightly.

They didn't return to the yacht. She already had her stuff and they climbed into a helicopter to be returned to Rhodes. They parted at the airport because Jace was boarding his private jet there to fly to Japan. A limo stuffed with security guards ferried her home, cleared a path through the shouting, aggressive mob on her doorstep and saw her indoors, where she found her father waiting.

'I used my key and came straight inside because I'd prefer not to be identified,' Achilleus Georgiou announced with an apologetic wince. 'I've been waiting, hoping you would return. I went to the shelter first but your boss told me that you wouldn't be coming in to work for a while.'

On edge as she always was with her father, Gigi was already lifting the post he had set on the table to examine it. There was a letter from her solicitor and she tore it open, wondering if her mother's property had finally found a buyer.

'Is it true? Are you engaged to Jace Diamandis? It was a shock to see a picture of you at their family party,' the older man admitted.

'We're not engaged. That was just a stupid misunderstanding,' Gigi volunteered tightly. 'But we are still seeing each other.'

Even her ability to make that modest claim eased the raw tension that had begun to build inside her the night before when Jace had let her go to bed alone. And then he had kissed her again and the breach between them had been healed with sincerity. Her sense of relief was so extreme that it scared her even more. She was falling in love with Jace Diamandis. She didn't want to but it was already happening in a process that had begun very early on at that first dinner together on the yacht. That was when she had seen the male seething with emotion behind the smooth playboy façade.

'What's in the letter?' Achilleus asked, as keen as she was, it seemed, for a change of subject.

'When I came out here, I couldn't find a buyer for Mum's house because there was a problem with the tenant. Now that the tenant has moved out, there's an offer on the house and the buyer has discovered that there's still stuff stored in the attic. I never checked the attic,' she grumbled guiltily. 'Mum put her personal belongings in a storage locker before she rented the house out and I did sort through that. I'll have to go back to Oxford, accept the offer and empty the attic.'

'Is there no alternative?' her father prompted.

'No, I don't think so and, since I'm on leave, it's best handled now. I didn't even know that Mum had ever used the attic!'

'I never thought I'd see my daughter at a swanky Diamandis party,' Achilleus confessed at the back door, from which he was hoping to make an unnoticed departure. 'You looked like a little queen, standing beside his grandmother... I was proud of you. Sorry I said what I did when I first knew you were seeing him. He's treating you with respect and I think the better of him for that.'

'Yes.' Gigi smiled up at him, for once at ease with the older man, even catching a glimmer of warmth in his dark eyes and heartened by it.

Gigi closed her front curtains, ignored the knocking on the front door and set about tidying and cleaning the house because she was restless. She phoned Thea to request a couple of weeks off and gained her agreement. She texted Jace to tell him she was travelling home to sort out some property hassles and asked if Hoppy and Tilly could stay on *Sea King* until her return. He phoned her to offer her the use of his private jet and she said no, thanks, and then he demanded to know where she would be staying and suggested that she use his property in London.

'I was going to book into a hotel.' A *cheap* hotel, she acknowledged, because even though her mother's property would be vacant, it had very little furniture and it wouldn't be worth buying bed linen and all the other things she would need to spend only a few nights there.

'Use my apartment,' Jace urged. 'I'd prefer that. I'd know that you were there and safe.'

Gigi parted her lips to argue again and then asked herself why she would argue. That he wanted to know she was safe and comfortable was reassuring. Not since childhood had anyone worried about Gigi's safety and comfort. 'OK.'

'And the jet?'

'Don't push it,' she told him drily.

Jace laughed. 'You'll be picked up off your flight and we'll have that blood test done while you're in London. Send me your flight details.'

Having booked her flight, Gigi relaxed a little. It would be a relief to finally settle her mother's estate. Once the house was sold, she would have the money to consider buying her own property on Rhodes. After all, her grandmother's house would eventually sell and she would have to find somewhere else to live. With her relatives on the island and closer friends than she had retained in the UK, that impressed her as a good plan. When had she stopped making such plans? When had she settled into a routine of only work and more work? Jace had sprung her out of that rut, but the price of their relationship would ultimately cost her dearly, she reflected unhappily. Nothing this good lasted for ever and she would be hurt.

Three days later she was collected by a limo at the airport in London and wafted back to a penthouse apartment. She was shown into a spacious, comfortable bedroom and served with an evening meal in the chic dining area off the large airy lounge with its views of the city. Breakfast awaited her when she rose early and a car arrived to ferry her to Oxford. The small, detached house that had belonged to her mother had few childhood associations for Gigi. She had vague memories of the rooms when they were still furnished but she had never climbed the folding metal stair that led up to the loft.

'Let us take a look first, Miss Campbell,' her driver and his companion urged, having already opened the hatch door for her to access the space.

Gigi let them climb up ahead of her and report back that there were only a few small pieces of old furniture and a couple of boxes. They brought the boxes down and she leafed through one, finding old files of her mother's and setting them aside to dump. The second box was more interesting, and she worked through it much more slowly because it contained family photos that she had never seen before as well as a photo of her actual parents posing together in sunlight, her mother smiling as she had so rarely smiled. There were old letters from people she had never heard of and right at the very bottom she found a dozen unopened letters that had been posted from Rhodes.

Her brow furrowed because she recognised her father's handwriting. Why were his letters to her mother unopened? The postal dates spanned the first six years of her life. Had an earlier letter from Achilleus angered her parent into rejecting all communication with him? Shaking her head over her mother's inflexibility, she tucked away the photos and the letters but she already knew that she wouldn't open her father's private letters. She would return them to him and perhaps that would prompt him to talk about the past and answer her questions, she reasoned.

When she rang Jace that evening, she told him about the letters. His attitude was very different from hers. He would have opened them.

'No, I'll be diplomatic and hand them back to him, see what he says,' Gigi argued. 'They're addressed to Mum and weren't meant for me to read.'

'It's your decision,' Jace sighed.

As soon as Gigi had organised the removal of the remaining furniture through a man who did house clearances, she visited the solicitor to sign the sale documents. It felt final and she was sad at the awareness that visiting her mother's former home had liberated no fond memories that she might have cherished. But then her mother had rarely given her daughter personal time. They had only ever shared occasional moments before her mother left on another business trip or Gigi returned to school. And her mother's main interest in her only child had always been limited to Gigi's academic achievements.

Late afternoon, Gigi went to the laboratory Jace had designated and agreed to a blood test taken from her arm. My goodness, she thought in sudden dismay, what if the result were to be positive? It would blow her entire future to pieces and set her on a totally different path. For the first time, she thought of how her mother had prioritised her career over family and she felt light-headed, acknowledging that, for a single parent, one's profession was all the more important when it came to financial security. Had she been a little harsh in her judgement of her mother? Even if she hadn't been loved, she had been well looked after. She breathed in deep. Her career was her security, she reminded herself. Helping animals validated her in a way family life had failed to do. No doubt she would deal with the upheaval if she was pregnant, she told herself firmly, refusing to let her fears and insecurities creep in. How would Jace react *if...*?

She refused to let herself sink into that craven state of anxiety. Wasn't it bad enough that she was twisting and turning in her bed every night remembering what it was like to be with him? She was reliving steamy moments and discovering that the sensual side he had awakened did not tidily go to sleep when he wasn't available. He was phoning her every day and it still wasn't enough. She was missing him more than she had believed it possible for her to miss anyone. Grow up, she told herself sternly. She was obsessing about Jace and it was unhealthy. And she would pay for it all in the future when he inevitably lost interest. Irritated by her state of mind, she contacted two university pals she had done internships with and suggested going for a drink the following evening to catch up.

'I can just call an Uber,' Gigi protested the next day when Jace's driver insisted that he needed to drop her off wherever she was going and Stavros, the beefy bodyguard, announced that he would be keeping her within view at all times. 'It really isn't necessary.'

'Mr Diamandis decides what's necessary,' Stavros responded. 'Perhaps you should mention it to him…but please don't quote me on that.'

Gigi gave up the argument and resolved to speak to Jace when she was dropped off at the bar. She had barely stepped onto the pavement when she was hailed by voices from an outside table. Glancing over, she saw Edison rolling his eyes at her and Marion staring at her with wide eyes.

She had forgotten that Edison was a chain smoker and always sat outside and she was grateful that she had a warm coat on because it was late October and, although it was dry, the breeze was icy.

'Gigi.' Edison stood up, his long, lanky frame towering over her. 'You've finally grown up. I can't believe it—'

'I think you're shooting for the moon here trying

to chat her up when she arrives in a chauffeur-driven car!' Marion quipped and stood up, a small no-nonsense woman with wildly curly hair and warm brown eyes. 'But Ed's right. It's been four years. At my wedding, you still looked like a kid and now all of a sudden you're an adult like the rest of us.'

Accepting a brief hug, Gigi took a seat and ordered a drink while Stavros seated himself close to the entrance. 'So, you're a mum now,' she said to Marion. 'What's it like?'

'If you're going to talk kids, I'm out of here,' Edison threatened.

'What's it like?' Marion looked heavenward. 'Overwhelming and terrifying and wonderful and all at the same time and often on the same day.'

Talk about work and their various specialities took over. Edison worked almost exclusively with horses but Marion was like Gigi, keener on dealing with smaller animals and pets. She was talking about the rescue centre when Marion answered her phone and almost instantly stood up and gathered up her bag. 'I'm going to have to cut and run. Damien has a fever and Steve is panicking,' she told them apologetically. 'Keep in touch, Gigi.'

'Looks like it's just the two of us.' Edison smirked at her and snaked an arm round her.

Gigi shook off his touch like a bristling cat. 'I should leave too,' she said wryly, reaching for her bag.

'Oh, come on, you're not that innocent these days…

not when you're running around with an infamous Greek playboy,' he told her with amusement, catching a thick hank of her hair in his hand to prevent her from moving. 'I fancied you like mad when we were working together but you were way too young and naïve—'

'Unfortunately, I don't fancy you any more,' Gigi told him furiously. 'I have a boyfriend and I don't cheat—'

'You heard her...let go of her,' a masculine, achingly familiar voice interposed from behind her.

Gigi almost pulled her hair out of her scalp twisting to look behind her in disbelief. *'Jace?'*

Jace tugged her hair firmly free of Edison's hold and literally lifted her out of her seat, both arms wrapped round her as though she were a parcel. *'Any more?'* he questioned as Stavros pulled open the door of the limo and he settled her on the passenger seat.

Gigi was on a high. Jace was here with her in London and she didn't know whether she was on her head or her heels, only that suddenly life felt wonderful and full to the brim with exciting possibilities again. 'I had a monster crush on Edison when I worked with him three years ago but nothing ever happened between us. I'm sure he guessed but I wasn't the pushy, flirtatious type,' she revealed, her cheeks heating at the memory as Jace vaulted in beside her. 'Why didn't you tell me you'd be coming?'

'I wanted to surprise you...wasn't expecting to get a surprise myself and find some jerk coming on to you!' he admitted, arranging his long-limbed length in a relaxed sprawl in the other corner of the back seat. 'Especially one that yanks at your hair to imprison you when you clearly don't want to be touched. He's lucky I didn't thump him!'

Gigi collided with black-lashed witch-green eyes and simply succumbed to temptation. She scrambled across the seat separating them like a homing pigeon. 'I missed you so much!' she groaned, burying her face in the shoulder of his coat, drinking in the ocean-fresh scent of him as though it were an addictive drug.

Jace locked two powerful arms round her and held her close. 'I missed you too, more than I wanted to, more than I expected to...you've got under my skin.'

Gigi finally lifted her head and looked down at him. Her mouth fell open. 'You've cut your beautiful hair!' she wailed, slender fingers threading forlornly through the cropped black hair. 'I *loved* your curls.'

'I thought it was time for a change.'

'You should've discussed it first.'

'Are you serious?'

'I'll go out tomorrow and get my hair cut to two inches long all over and see how you like it!' Gigi threatened.

Jace gazed up at her with a spellbinding smile tilting his wide, sensual mouth. 'I can see that being one half of even a temporary couple involves rules,' he murmured wickedly. 'It's time I started making some. No meeting up with other men when I'm not around—'

'Are you the jealous type?' Gigi asked with interest.

Her blue eyes were sparkling with considerable amusement and faint dark colour edged his sculpted cheekbones.

'I didn't used to be, but I don't like seeing another man put his hands on any part of you...most especially not without your permission.' Long, lean fingers threaded through her wind-tousled hair, spanned the base of her skull and drew her head down.

Her heart was racing so fast she was breathless with anticipation. He crushed her parted lips beneath his. He was hungry, urgent, demanding in flavour and it was exactly what she most wanted and needed to satisfy the hollow ache inside her. Unfortunately, it only whetted her appetite for more, her hands sliding below his coat and running down his shirt-clad sides, yanking at the fine cotton to reach skin. He flexed his hips up and she felt him hard and long and thick through the barrier of their clothes and lust almost ate her alive.

Jace sat up fast, his hands biting into her hips as he lifted and steadied her. 'Not here, not in the car.' He dropped a kiss on the crown of her head and she felt his lean, taut frame shudder against her. 'You could make me as reckless as a teenager, *koukla mou*,' he groaned, setting her beside him on the seat and belting her in.

'It's been a long week,' she mumbled, shamefaced that he had called a halt before she had.

He closed a hand over her smaller one. 'Did you go for that blood test?'

'Yes. I should get a call tomorrow,' she told him

stiffly, finding it impossible not to tense when it came to discussing *that* controversial subject. 'I still think you're worrying about nothing.'

'We'll see.'

They made it as far as the private lift up to the penthouse and he grabbed her and kissed her with all the hungry urgency he had earlier restrained. Plastered to each other, they exchanged kiss for kiss, their tongues duelling, their bodies tangling so that he carried her out of the lift and down to the main bedroom. Gigi was quivering, every nerve-ending screaming with excitement, her heart hammering when he laid her down on the bed and stood over her, tipping off his coat, wrenching his tie off, toeing off his shoes, appraising her with fierce impatience.

'Yes, you definitely did miss me,' Gigi murmured with unconcealed satisfaction as he yanked her free of her jeans.

'I almost got ravished in the limo,' Jace traded smugly. 'You're unlikely to win a who-missed-who-most competition. I was shocked rigid by your enthusiasm, Miss Campbell. Only weeks ago, you were an innocent virgin.'

Gigi came up on her knees. 'Shut up,' she told him, reaching up to undo his belt and run his zip down because he wasn't stripping fast enough for her.

And then he was in her arms again as he had not been in days and everything in her world seemed to slot perfectly back into place again, as though he were the missing piece of her personal puzzle. The heat of him, the strength of his long, lean frame, the scent of him, the touch of him, all of it engulfed her like a tidal wave. His mouth on hers, his hand on her breast, the urgency of his answering arousal against her stomach drove her higher in the sky than a kite. Her heartbeat crashed inside her, thundered in her ears as Jace dug out protection and thrust deep inside her, joining them in the intimacy she craved. Nothing had ever been more exciting than that exact moment when she gazed up into his striking green eyes and realised that she truly loved him to a level she had never realised she could love anyone.

Jace stilled in the aftermath, both arms still solidly locked round her. He didn't want to let go of her yet. Nothing wrong with that, he assured himself, not considering how much he had missed her. He supposed it was an infatuation and he was overdue for the experience, but he reckoned that he would never ever admit to his uncle that a relationship could be so much more exciting than casual, uncommitted sex. Evander had lived long enough to already know that as a fact. But *naturally*, Jace, who was still *only* twenty-eight, would bounce back from this total immersion experience with *one* woman and want his freedom of choice back, he told himself without hesitation. He wasn't interested in a permanent relationship, not when his own history warned him of how dangerously unstable and messy such entanglements could become.

In the middle of the night, Gigi lurched out of bed

and made snacks for them from what she found in the well-stocked fridge. 'When do you start back to work again?' she heard herself ask, dismayed by the anxiety that gripped her at the idea of him leaving her again.

'I'm working here for a couple of days, sleeping off the jet lag, spending time with you,' he framed lazily, lounging back against the kitchen island while he ate. He resembled a pin-up model, clad only in black boxers and his dazzling smile, all the lean, muscular, bronzed, hair-roughened beauty of him on full display.

And he still, at a mere glance, she acknowledged guiltily, stole the very breath from her lungs. There wasn't much she could do about that. She would see it through until the end and ensure that it finished without recriminations and with dignity. That was the only promise she made to herself.

'I miss the pets,' she confided.

'Of course you do, and you even had to part with two of them on Faros, but we'll be back in Rhodes in forty-eight hours,' he reminded her. 'And I've no doubt there are more Gigi rescues in your future—'

'I haven't much space. Once the money from Mum's house clears, I'm planning to buy somewhere with at least a small garden attached. My grandmother's house where I'm living will ultimately sell.'

'Stay with me on the yacht, instead,' Jace urged.

Gigi paled and tensed at that suggestion. 'Not a good idea for us to be blurring the lines that way—'

'What's that supposed to mean?' Jace demanded

starkly, his big shoulders straightening and lifting, all relaxation abandoned.

Gigi's mouth ran dry and she shrugged awkwardly. 'I don't want to be depending on you for the roof over my head when we break up.'

'Thank you,' Jace breathed with lashings of sarcasm. 'As a thought for the day on the same day that we *re-unite*, that is kind of depressing.'

Gigi wrinkled her nose in semi-agreement. 'But realistic.'

Jace gritted his teeth on the truth that only hours earlier he had been thinking the same way, but the very concept of Gigi walking away, retaining her independence… Gigi with other men…still drove him crazy. He still hated rebuffs. Rejection always sucked him back to his birth parents' negative treatment of him.

He breathed in slow and deep and said nothing because he couldn't think of what he could say in the face of Gigi's immensely gloomy but intelligent practicality. He lived in the moment. Gigi lived on a much wider plane, foreseeing problems that didn't even occur to him. Did that mean that she was more mature than he was? a dark little voice whispered inside him and he immediately suppressed that suspicion. Much the same as he had done with the suspicion that, had she been a different kind of woman, she was clever enough to have run rings round him.

Hours later, Jace groaned. 'That's your phone, not mine. Switch it off,' he urged.

Gigi rolled naked out of bed in the daylight filtering through the curtains and dug through the pile of clothes spread across the floor to find her jeans and answer her phone.

'Miss Campbell?' the polite voice began. 'This is a confidential call. Could you give me your details before I give you the test result?'

It was the laboratory. As Gigi answered the questions to prove her identity, she paused. Jace had sat up in bed, shrewd eyes as green as polished emeralds pinned to her sudden pallor and the tension etched in her fine-boned features. A minute later she pushed the phone back into the pocket of her jeans.

'I'm pregnant,' she whispered shakily in total shock and denial, perspiration breaking out on her brow.

CHAPTER EIGHT

AND WHAT SHOOK Jace the most in that moment was the inexcusably weird shot of satisfaction that rocketed through him and the even less presentable thought, Try walking away now…

He was shocked by his own reaction and wondered what the hell was happening to his brain. A…*baby*? He didn't know any, so had little to say on the subject, but for the first time in his life in recent weeks, and ever since the risk of a pregnancy had arisen, Jace had started noticing babies for the first time. Babies…and pregnant women. That curiosity had freaked him out a little even while it had somewhat acquainted him with the possibility of becoming a parent.

'*Pregnant!*' Gigi gasped, stricken.

'It's not the end of the world,' Jace pointed out, feeling remarkably calm in the crisis. 'Come back to bed. It's too early to get up—'

'Come back to bed?' Gigi repeated, studying him as though he had sprouted horns and cloven feet in his apparent madness. 'Are you crazy? After getting news like that?'

Jace vaulted out of bed and clasped her hand to tug her upright and off the rug where she was still sitting like a woman felled by a lightning bolt. 'We were up half the night. You're exhausted. This is not the time to talk about this—'

'It's a nightmare...' Gigi looked up at him with tears swimming in her eyes.

'We're not having a drama over this,' Jace assured her with innate confidence, bending down to scoop her off her bare feet and tuck her with care back into her side of the huge bed. 'You'll feel better once you've slept for a while and will be more able to deal with it—'

'I'm not having a termination!' she shot at him accusingly.

Jace stretched out an arm and edged her close in a determined movement. 'I don't want that either—'

'But what are we going to *do*?' Gigi snapped at him in frustration, because his complete inhuman cool was not at all how she had expected him to deal with such an announcement. She had assumed that he would be shaken, horrified, angry...all likely responses from a young, single guy, who was in no way ready or eager for fatherhood with a woman he had only recently met.

Inside himself, Jace was in shock as well at the prospect of becoming a parent and the lifelong commitment that would demand from him. His birth parents had been lousy at the job, he acknowledged, little better than disinterested bystanders during his early childhood. He would have to do a hell of a lot better on that front than they had. But right now, he couldn't afford to reveal his panic to Gigi because it would only fuel hers. No, he needed to take a deep breath and step back and come up with a solution. That meant *not* getting emotional or dramatising the situation. He needed to concentrate on the practicalities.

'We'll get married—'

'What?' Gigi shot bolt upright in the bed, almost elbowing him in the face in her disbelief as he too sat up again, looking very much put upon.

Jace surveyed her aghast expression, mentally leafed through all possible arguments and came up with the one most practical, most likely to appeal to her as a future parent. 'All the Diamandis family holdings are in a trust. For my firstborn to inherit his or her share, the parents have to be *married*. I doubt that either of us are sufficiently anti-matrimony to disinherit our future child because we can't be bothered tying the knot.'

Thoroughly disconcerted by that very rational and unemotional explanation, Gigi slowly lay down again. Jace relaxed then and curved her back into him. 'Go back to sleep. You're catastrophising… I can *feel* it. We're adults and we have nobody but ourselves to consider in this. We'll handle it together—'

'Do you really mean that?' Gigi muttered worriedly.

'Do you truly not trust me enough to accept my word?'

Marriage? Marry Jace? Yes, she could do it for the sake of their child's potential prosperity, she reasoned in a daze, thinking that she had no choice on *that* basis. But what had Jace done with all the emotion she had initially sensed seething in him when she first made that announcement? Where had it gone? He hadn't said one word wrong. Was he always that tactful? Why did she have the suspicion that he had gone undercover with his emotions like some stupid secret agent on a mission?

Gigi went to sleep. Jace expelled his breath in a discreet sigh of relief. A baby. He didn't know anything about babies, but he had seen one or two in prams in Japan that had struck him as being reasonably cute and interesting. None of his friends had a child. The Diamandis men, however, usually didn't marry until middle age and he would be breaking that cycle. He splayed a sneaky hand across Gigi's still flat stomach as she slumbered and he swore to that tiny life inside her that he would be a much better father than his birth parents had been to him.

Challenged, however, by the altered future now opening up ahead of him, Jace was restless. He slid quietly out of bed and went off to use his phone and share his news with his family. After all, it was his duty to control the narrative and ensuring that there were few surprises ahead would prevent him from dwelling on the emotional stuff.

Gigi wakened to having breakfast served to her in bed, Jace straightening to tower over her, fully dressed in a designer elegant suit. He looked stupendous even first thing in the morning and she knew that she did not, not without a brush through her hair, her teeth clean—and even some pyjamas would not have gone amiss. She dropped her evasive gaze to the beautifully prepared tray and wondered uncertainly when and just how they had become so intimate. She had fallen for him like a ton of bricks but that didn't mean she had to be dependent on him...for anything. Indeed, Gigi had based her entire life to date on not needing anyone for anything because she could usually take care of herself better than anyone else.

'I've organised a doctor's appointment for you this morning.' Jace fell silent as Gigi lifted stunned eyes to his. 'He's a top obstetrician. I assumed that move was only sensible...to have you checked out because we haven't had that done yet—'

'I don't think there's any royal "we" when I'm the one who's pregnant,' Gigi heard herself say tartly, even though all the while an inner voice was urging her not to be a five-letter word of a woman when he was only trying to take care of her. The way nobody had *ever* taken care of her, she reminded herself ruefully. Maybe that was why her hackles were raised, because that kind of treatment was new to her and it gave her an almost threatened feel, which her intelligence warned her was a ridiculous response.

'Seeing a doctor is normal,' she agreed in addition, cheeks flushing as she made that concession, disliking the irrational resentments assailing her. It wasn't *his* fault that they were in this predicament. If anything, it was *her* fault for not having taken the contraceptive precautions most young women in her age group did. Her fault for assuming that she would never meet a guy she wanted to have sex with. How realistic had that conviction been? For goodness' sake, he was standing right there now beside her and a dangerous, reckless and wanton part of her still wanted to drag him down on the bed and rip him back out of that business suit. He stole her self-control; he changed her into someone she felt uncomfortable with.

Sadly, she didn't seem to have the same effect on him. His shrewd and striking green eyes were impassive, his lean, dark, devastating face calm as a tranquil sea. *Businesslike?* She didn't know the side of Jace he was currently giving her and it…unnerved her more than a little. Not to know what he was thinking or feeling left her feeling shut out, distanced, and he hadn't given her one typical, normal extrovert Jace reaction since she had uttered that fatal word 'pregnant' first thing that morning.

Jace had never wanted so badly to peel back the layers in a person and see exactly what went on inside their head. Gigi was freaking out, *still* freaking out about the baby and he didn't know what to do about that. He was trying to be supportive, and she didn't like that either. His even white teeth gritted hard in frustration. An efficient can-do approach towards the practicalities would surely soothe her as any emotional reaction would not.

'Eat something,' he urged, since she had yet to touch a crumb of the food on her tray.

All her favourite items were on the tray. When had he noticed exactly what she liked to eat? My word, they hadn't been together *that* long! But there sat the hot chocolate and the yogurt and the fruit like a statement. And she hadn't a clue what he preferred for breakfast! Did that make her a very selfish, useless girlfriend? Exasperated by the constant clamour of anxiety and insecurity assailing her without warning, Gigi began to eat and Jace backed off a few feet.

Showered and fresh, Gigi pulled on her jeans and a somewhat shabby sweater and studied herself in a mirror, feeling unusually critical of her appearance. She had to buy some clothes, she conceded ruefully, never having been a fan of shopping. But she had next to nothing left to wear in a true winter climate.

'Why so serious?' Jace chided, striding over to her as he pulled open the door into the lift.

'Well, it's all serious stuff now, isn't it?' she framed bleakly.

A lean hand curved to her tense jawline and Jace lowered his head to claim a kiss. Not a light kiss, not a 'comforting the little woman in the lift' kiss, a downright passionate claiming kiss that shook her inside out and made her toes curl in her scuffed winter ankle boots. She blinked up at him in astonishment as he walked her out to the waiting car. It was the first thing he had done since they learned of her pregnancy that revealed emotion and she loved it.

In the back of the car, he offered her a drink and she said no, thank you. In a speedy sleight of hand that thoroughly disconcerted her, Jace produced a glittering ring and threaded it with great care onto her engagement finger. 'Er...what's this?' she mumbled.

'You know it's an engagement ring because we're getting married,' Jace pointed out flatly.

'Of course...for the look of things, for appearances,' she mumbled, a stiletto knife piercing her heart as she surveyed the truly gorgeous ring that was pretty much a fake as far as his intentions were concerned. It wasn't huge, which she would have hated, but a delicate, creative swirl of dazzlingly bright diamonds that would undoubtedly have cost the earth and some change. 'It's really beautiful, Jace,' she extended unevenly. 'Very elegant and not too much for my small hand. Thank you.'

A little mollified, Jace studied her taut profile until he noticed that her lower lip was wobbling as if she was on the brink of tears. 'What's wrong?'

What was wrong was that she could hardly tell him that she wished the ring and the supposed sentiments attached to it were real instead of fake to make them look like a genuine engaged couple. 'Nothing... I don't know what's the matter with me,' she said truthfully. 'I feel weepy and that's not normal for me.'

'It's probably stress. I don't want you stressing about *anything*,' Jace informed her in a forceful undertone. 'If there's any stressing to be done, let it be my problem, rather than yours. Evander and Marcus and my grandmother will take care of the wedding on Faros. All you have to do is choose your gown.'

Gigi swivelled in her seat in dismay. 'The wedding?' she gasped. 'You're *already* making arrangements for it?'

Jace dealt a sizzling appraisal. 'Why not? Since we're doing it, there's little point in waiting.'

With difficulty, Gigi held her tongue. She felt trapped, harassed, pushed into choices she had barely had time to consider. But was that reasonable? Hadn't she agreed to marry him? For the sake of their child's future inheritance? Which sounded horrendous, she acknowledged. Surely more should come into the decision than something so reliant on cold, hard cash?

'We probably won't like being married,' she warned him stiffly, while thinking that she would cope fine with the prospect of having him almost every day, *but* he had always been accustomed to more adventurous possibilities: fabulous underwear models, gorgeous screen stars, polished socialites. His past contained all of those options and how could she possibly compare?

'We'll manage,' Jace pronounced in a tone of finality.

Gigi went through the prior tests for her appointment at the surgery before Jace joined her in the consulting room and the obstetrician, a suave male in his forties or so, gave her an ultrasound to show them the tiny blip of their child inside her. The backs of her eyes stung with happy tears. Jace brushed her cheekbone to wipe away that bead of moisture when it trickled down without her noticing.

'I know, *asteri mou*,' he breathed soft and low. 'It's pretty special.'

He was calling her 'my star' and she almost wept all over him at the affectionate term. But that was *before* Mr Eames, the consultant, learned that she was a veterinary surgeon and revealed that his wife was one as well and that she had given up work for the duration of each of her pregnancies.

'Was that really necessary?' Jace asked in surprise.

'Toxic chemicals, dangerous procedures, the risk of infection or harm from an injured animal…what do *you* think?' the older man responded.

'Perhaps your wife works more with livestock than I do,' Gigi said stiffly even as her brain was spiralling with horror at the mere thought of not being able to work. Work had always been her holy grail, her anchor, what she based her whole life on. The threat of being without her job terrified her.

'Even so, there are a lot of risks for a pregnant woman in your field. Will you really take that chance with your baby?' the consultant prompted. 'Of course, if you're part of a big practice, your colleagues can handle the patients you can't…that would work.'

But Gigi didn't have that option. There was nobody else at the rescue shelter able to perform her job. Ioanna was qualified to do vaccinations and blood tests

but that was about it. It would require another vet to do
the surgeries and some other treatments. Her troubled
eyes veiled and her slight frame stiffened.

'So, you quit for a few months,' Jace remarked without any expression at all as he tucked her back into the
limousine.

Gigi's eyes widened but she said nothing because
the prospect of losing her job was like a crack of doom
sounding above her head that reverberated through her
entire body. It was her security, her very foundation.
She was going to lose everything that mattered to her,
she reflected in a frantic, fearful surge of anxiety. Her
whole life would fall apart without work.

'That's easy for you to say. It's not that simple,' she
objected.

'Nothing about this situation is easy for either of us,'
Jace countered drily.

And her heart sank to her boot soles because that was
finally telling her, wasn't it? That all his careful plans
were against his personal wishes? That he didn't want
the baby or her and certainly didn't want to marry her?
Gigi swallowed very hard and, in containing herself,
she went rigid.

'What's wrong?' Jace asked in the lift on the way
back up to the apartment.

'How can you ask me that?' she hissed at him, her
messy emotions finally breaking through to the surface.
'My life is about to fall apart at the seams!' she shot at
him in the foyer of the apartment.

'This is about your job, isn't it?' Jace murmured flatly, studying her the way a male might have studied a grenade about to blow.

'Full marks for perception!' Gigi gasped as she stalked down the bedroom corridor to their room to blow up in solo privacy.

Regrettably, Jace, it seemed, could not take a hint that just at that moment she was better left alone to deal with unwelcome medical advice. She felt as if the top of her head were about to blow off with anger and frustration. But Jace, cool as always, strolled in, closed the door and leant back against it. He looked almost insanely hot and sexy. Her breasts peaked under her sweater and something in her pelvis tightened right then, doubly infuriating her. It was bad enough having pulled the short straw with her pregnancy and marriage to a guy who didn't want *either* of them, but it felt like betraying herself to still want him so badly.

'Tell me what's wrong,' Jace murmured. 'I can fix most things—'

'You can't fix *this*!'

'Do you want this child?' Jace asked with lethal quietness, bright green eyes narrowed to an intimidating degree, and it was yet another side of Jace that she had not seen before. For a split second, he chilled her where she stood.

'No...no, it's not that,' she declared, devastated by that question, shocked he would ask because, of course, her baby was more important to her than her job. 'The baby's here and it's staying inside me until it's born. It's everything else…this wedding—'

'Which you agreed to,' he interposed drily.

'The impact the pregnancy will have on my working life. I mean, there would be risks I would have to avoid—'

'We'll get better advice, *qualified* advice,' Jace incised. 'And if it's still a potential problem I will cover the cost of another vet working with you—'

'For goodness' sake, you can't buy everything!' Gigi launched at him with scorn.

'I will pay for virtually anything that makes you happier,' Jace told her levelly, wondering why she didn't recognise how hard he was trying to shape the future into something that she could accept. 'That's not extravagance or foolishness when I'm your future husband, it's my duty.'

That word, 'duty', hit Gigi like a brick smashing through glass. 'Oh, take a hike, Jace. Leave me alone to get my head straight. I'm sorry. I'm in a bad mood. And it doesn't help *that*—' Her voice broke off. 'No, never mind.'

'Never mind about what? *What* doesn't help?' he pressed grimly, knowing that he dared not respond in a similar emotional way lest he lose control of the situation and made a mess of calming her down.

'That you're not giving me an honest, genuine answer to *anything*!' Gigi fired back at him, unable to silence that frightening conviction. 'I feel like all I'm being told is what you think *I* want to hear and that's not fair to either of us right now! I don't want to be manipulated like that. I can take bad news like any other woman!'

'I'm not manipulating you. I'm trying to keep you calm because I don't imagine it's good for you right now to get so upset,' Jace declared without hesitation, determined not to react. She was having his baby and he would do whatever it took to smooth that journey for her. Much good it would do them if he went off in an emotional scene and accelerated hers!

'Because I'm pregnant,' Gigi guessed, and she still wanted to slap him, slap him and drag him back into bed at the same time. But no, that wasn't where he was at in this moment. He was too busy suffering through a *scary* pregnant woman experience and handling her with velvet gloves like a dangerous science experiment. 'You're taking that far too seriously. As you said, it's not the end of the world,' she proffered, hoping to draw him out.

'You're the one still behaving as though it is the end of the world, so why are you questioning my behaviour?' Jace asked, logical down to the bone.

'That's not what I'm talking about!' Gigi flung back at him with spirit. 'I'm talking about the fact that you don't feel able to be honest with me any more and I can't stand that… It's like there's a wall between us now!'

Striding back to the door, Jace angled a scorching look like live green fire at her, his cut jaw line taut and hard. 'I don't know what I'm supposed to say. I don't do the touchy-feely stuff with women, if that's what you're expecting. Maybe it's because I'm a guy or maybe it's because… I'm emotionally repressed—'

'Or maybe it's because you're a coward and can't face the challenge of honesty,' Gigi interposed stiffly, aware that he was on the brink of losing his temper, wanting to push that, *not* wanting to push that in equal parts. Indeed, she was not even sure quite what she *did* want from him. All she really knew was that she felt torn apart and weak with insecurity and fear and that that, more than anything else, was what she wanted him to fix for her.

In the corridor, Jace stopped dead as though faced with a loaded gun and then he swung back to her, dazzling green eyes chilling as a polar freeze. 'Do you think you could strive to handle this situation with a little more maturity?'

It was Gigi's turn to ice over, knees stiffening beneath her to brace her and keep her taut back straight. 'Obviously you don't think so,' she parried.

'You say that you want honesty but, believe me…*you don't,*' Jace gritted, staring at her, wondering what had happened to the woman who had bewitched him without even trying to do so. Him? Was it his own fault? Was he supposed to lie down like a rug for her to walk over? Too bad, that brand of weakness wasn't in the Diamandis DNA. He could not recall ever being so angry with anyone and certainly not a woman, but at the same time he knew that he could not bear to utter a single word that she might take wrong. They could talk *after* the wedding, when all the fuss was over, when it was only the two of them and the baby news had settled in with her. So, he wasn't splashing his emotions round the place as she was…but that wasn't his job right now. She needed him to be sensible and controlled and consider the greater good.

'So you say.' With difficulty, refusing to show her vulnerability, Gigi simply shrugged a slight shoulder. Hadn't her own mother warned her times without number that men ducked out when the going got tough? Warned her that she had to be hard and independent and trust in no one other than herself? And from no age at all, Gigi had learned to live that way.

'Grow up, *glykia mou*,' Jace advised with icy restraint. 'Our baby comes first and we must learn to compromise for our child's benefit. That's the bottom line and agonising over it won't change it.'

And with that final uncompromising dressing-down, Jace strode off and Gigi backed into the bedroom again, sick at heart and even her tummy churning. Funny how the obstetrician had asked her if she had suffered any nausea and she had said no and now, all of a sudden, she felt sick as a dog. It wasn't funny, she acknowledged, lying down on the bed, wishing that Jace would come back and simply put his arms round her.

It was as though he had not the smallest idea of how much difference that one little gesture could make at a tense time. And was she likely to be the one to teach him? She, whose mother had never once hugged her, who herself had only ever shown affection to Jace? But possibly his omission was more honest than his words had been. She was hugging him because she was crazy in love with him. Why would he think to hug her in the midst of their current plight?

So, what kind of marriage was it likely to be? Gigi wiped her tears away. *Our* baby, he had said for the very first time. She supposed that label had finally answered all the questions he had refused to answer. He would marry her for their child's sake and not for any other reason.

When she rose after a sleepless night, it was to a text on her phone, informing her that Jace had flown to New York on business, apologising for the change of plan and for the necessity of her returning to Greece alone.

And now, she had contrived to drive him away, she thought wretchedly. Could she really blame him, though, for not wanting to spell out truths that, in all honesty, she did not want to hear?

CHAPTER NINE

ELECTRA DIAMANDIS TWITCHED the Elizabethan stand-up collar of Gigi's wedding dress straight and stepped back, beaming with satisfaction. 'You look beautiful, Gigi. You have classic taste.'

Gigi flushed. No, she didn't, she had simply fallen in love after trying on a welter of big bouffant dresses that swallowed her small stature alive. And the one she had chosen was a simple sheath with long sleeves, an up-standing beaded decorative collar and a narrow skirt that flattered her height and shape. The bodice was beaded with intricate rose designs. The costly fabric was pure silk with the weight to drop into elegant folds. And the colour was pure white because Electra had had very firm ideas about what even Jace's pregnant bride should wear and it hadn't been the ivory tint that Gigi had initially assumed would be expected of her.

Yes, the past two weeks had been a breathtaking whirl of surprises, shocks and constant activity, all shared with Jace's family while her future husband stayed safe from the bridal madness on the other side of the world. Evander and Electra had taken her to a designer salon to choose her gown. The wedding would take place on the island of Faros at the Diamandis home.

Humphrey the tortoise now rejoiced in a purpose-built cave and pond complex in the garden. He was living the life of one in a million tortoises and the perfect life for a very lazy one. Snowy was enjoying an equally fabulous existence in Electra's private quarters being hand-fed nuts and he was slowly beginning to speak. Retrieved from the yacht, her own pets were revelling in luxury as well. Currently, Tilly was sunbathing indolently out on the balcony beyond the bedroom. Mo and Hoppy were curled up together in a corner, having greeted Gigi's return with rapture and shared her bed ever since.

Her otherwise *empty* bed. She had not seen Jace since that last day in London and she was not quite sure that she believed that genuinely urgent business had demanded his long absence. She blamed herself, she totally blamed herself for exploding their developing relationship. She had wanted more than he was offering her, *so much more*, she conceded sadly, the sort of stuff a guy couldn't give if he wasn't in love. And Jace was not in love with her. She had come to terms with that, she reminded herself doggedly. They had very good reasons to marry for their child's benefit, not least the loving support of Jace's immediate family.

It had been a shock to arrive on Faros and discover that everybody already *knew* that she was carrying Jace's baby. He had told the lot of them, demonstrating a lack of discretion that had astounded Gigi. Electra, Evander and Marcus, however, could hardly contain their delight over the news, which she had to admit had been heartwarming in a manner to which she was unaccustomed for she had yet to share that same news with her own Greek relatives. Jace might hail from a dysfunctional background but the family who had stood by him at the age of six were still fully present for him... and very supportive of his bride-to-be. She was deeply grateful for that family warmth and unquestioning acceptance that had never come her way before.

She had chosen to invite her Greek family to her wedding. Leaving them out would only have hurt and offended her father. Achilleus, her stepmother, Katerina, and her half-brothers had travelled to Faros on *Sea King* to meet Jace's family. Understandably, they had been overwhelmed by the experience of the yacht, the house's grandeur and their welcoming hosts. Katerina had tactfully sidestepped the invite to help dress Gigi for her big day, recognising that she and her stepdaughter didn't yet stand on such close terms, and that thoughtfulness had convinced Gigi that she had made the right decision. Besides, the attitude of her father's wife had been so much warmer and friendlier than Gigi had dimly assumed it would be that she was now pretty certain that that relationship was set to improve.

As for the fuss over Gigi's career having to be put on hold for her pregnancy—that had turned out to be a silly storm in a teacup, a storm that Gigi now very much regretted setting off with Jace by being too precious and pessimistic. The day after she had freaked out in the wake of the obstetrician's advice, she had gone to see one of her former professors at university. And the truth was that, yes, she would have to take extra care, glove up, be cautious, but in a small animal practice there was no reason why she shouldn't work as late into her pregnancy as she chose to do. Given that safety procedures and risk assessments were respected, she would be fine.

'That's marvellous,' Jace had pronounced flatly when she had apologetically shared that welcome clarification with him on the phone. 'We'll use the yacht as a base so that you can remain close to Rhodes.'

And now into the bargain she had been invited to become one of the directors on the board of the charity that ran the animal shelter because of Jace's massive donation to their funds. In short, in the space of weeks, her life had evolved to an extent that she could never have foreseen while she was over in London. Indeed, life would have been perfect if she were not still cherishing such very strong feelings for Jace. After all, other people seemed to manage detached, unemotional relationships with partners. Why couldn't she be the same?

Why did she have to miss Jace every hour of every day? Why did she shiver just hearing his voice on the phone? Why did she lie in bed wishing he were with her with every fibre of her being? All that excess feeling in Jace's direction worried Gigi. Where had that inner intensity been hidden for the twenty-three years that had preceded Jace's appearance in her life? Now she was subject to emotions that felt too powerful to suppress or fully control. And in the future she would need to control her possessive, almost obsessive love for Jace. How loyal would he be behind closed doors to a wife he didn't love? He was twenty-eight, not fifty-eight, nowhere near any nominal age when sexual temptation might be deemed to be a little less potent.

Early on the morning of her wedding day, Gigi anchored a small hand to her father's arm as they stood at the foot of the aisle in the church.

His brother, Nic, by his side, Jace awaited her at the altar. He was tall, dark, startlingly handsome in profile. She could see that his hair had grown and started to curl again since their last meeting and a helpless smile put to flight her anxious expression because he looked so much more familiar: he looked like *her* Jace again. In almost the same moment, primed by the swelling notes of the organ music, Jace swung fully round and dazzling jewelled eyes locked to her as she moved towards him.

In the candlelit interior, Gigi took his breath away in that dress with diamonds sparkling in her hair and her ears. It had been the longest two weeks of Jace's life but suddenly it all seemed worth it. The dramas, the misunderstandings, the uncharacteristic restraint of having to bite his tongue. It had all been for the greater good to bring them to this moment when the future opened up and enclosed them both. Looking at Gigi, he decided it was definitely worth it. They might still have a load of issues to work through, but he knew he wanted her as his wife more than he wanted anything else in the world.

Gigi drowned in the burning intensity of Jace's appraisal. A full body shiver of awareness racked her slender body. That raw, seething intensity that was uniquely Jace got to her every time. For a timeless moment, all her worries disappeared, and it was just her and him, the packed church surrounding them forgotten.

'You look stunning,' Jace informed her before the priest began to speak.

A faint flush of warmth infiltrated Gigi's exposed skin. Her heart hammered, her pulses quickened and she snatched in a faint steadying breath. She felt her nipples prickle and push against the boned bodice of her dress, felt the tightening inner muscles clench in her pelvis. Embarrassment gripped her as she fought to concentrate on the ceremony. Some minutes later, she looked down in faint consternation at the wedding ring that Jace eased onto her finger because, for an instant, it didn't seem possible that they could be married. Only as Jace helped her to slide a heavier version of her ring over his knuckle did it dawn on her that in this, at least, it was real. For better or for worse and certainly on paper, they were now husband and wife.

As they climbed into the waiting vintage car, which was festooned in flowers, Jace curved an arm to her spine and whispered, 'It feels like a hundred years since I was with you in London.'

For a split second, Gigi was tempted to quip that she was sure that he had been glad to have an excuse to escape a woman ready to call him a coward for his reluctance to be honest about how he truly felt about her. But with hindsight, everything that had happened between them had since mysteriously taken on a different guise. Why trash what they *could* have in favour of what she couldn't have? If a guy didn't love her, forcing him to admit that and admit that he didn't really want to be married to her would only create tension and bad feeling. Why on earth would she do that to them both?

So, it sucked to be her, to love and not be loved in return, but she wasn't the first woman to be in that position and definitely wouldn't be the last. She was more intelligent than that, she told herself fiercely. Perhaps it would be wiser to put the past behind her and focus on the future, focus on what she did have, rather than what she didn't.

'I missed you,' she conceded ruefully. 'But your family have been amazing.'

'What about your own? Make sure I meet them all at the reception,' Jace urged her. 'Have you confronted your father with those letters yet?'

'No, not yet.' Gigi frowned. 'I want to talk to him about that when we're somewhere private and I haven't had that chance yet. I'm not planning to *confront* him either…he hasn't done anything wrong—'

'Except withhold the truth about his relationship with your mother,' Jace reminded her drily.

'Mum did that first. I'll find the right time to talk to him and return those letters,' Gigi declared with confidence. 'But it won't be today at our wedding.'

'And not for the next couple of weeks either,' Jace forecast as he handed her out of the car outside the Diamandis house. 'We're honeymooning in Oman. Evander and Marcus are loaning us their holiday retreat in Muscat but we'll only be using it as a base. We'll be travelling around.'

'I wasn't expecting a honeymoon. I haven't asked to take any more time off,' Gigi muttered, her eyes wide with dismay.

'I organised it for you. Almost two weeks ago, I spoke to your boss and arranged for the shelter to retain your replacement until you return. You need a holiday, Gigi. As long as your work is covered, you're free as a bird.'

They moved indoors through the surge of bustling catering staff and walked out back to a shaded terrace where cold drinks were brought to them. Gigi started rising from her seat again to greet their arriving guests in the hall but Jace planted a staying hand on her knee. 'My family will handle them. We can enjoy five minutes alone,' he told her as he placed a jewellery box on her lap. 'Wedding gift.'

'You've already given me far more than you need to,' Gigi protested, colour lashing her cheeks as she thought of the entire wardrobe of clothes for all seasons that had crammed the dressing room upstairs. 'I mean, for goodness' sake, I'm wearing your grandmother's tiara, your mother's diamond earrings—'

'Those are family jewels. This is a personal gift from me to you,' Jace specified.

Gigi opened the box and lifted out a shimmering pendant. A diamond-studded wolfhound with golden eyes met her startled gaze.

'But for Mo, we wouldn't have met.' Striking green eyes levelly held her thoroughly disconcerted ones as he removed the item from her grasp and urged her to lower her head so that he could place it round her neck.

'Our first meeting wasn't exactly romantic,' Gigi protested even while she cherished the sheer shock value of Jace doing such a thing. He wasn't that type of guy, she could have sworn that he was not, yet…?

'But you warmed up to me,' Jace pointed out with a charismatic smile.

'An icicle would warm up to you,' Gigi mumbled, slender fingertips caressing the wolfhound pendant, but there was no hiding it: she was touched and impressed by a romantic gesture she had not expected from the once scarily honest male she had just married. 'It's absolutely gorgeous—'

'A perfect match for my absolutely gorgeous bride.' Jace sprang upright, offering her his arm. 'It's time for us to go public again. Shall we?'

The bridal celebrations and the crowds of guests swiftly engulfed them. As Jace finally guided her to the top table in the huge ballroom, one of his hands spanned her waist to ease her close. Bending his dark head, he ravished her parted lips slowly and thoroughly with his and whispered huskily, 'I can't wait until we're alone…only a few hours to get through now.'

As his lean, muscular body brushed against hers, her own blood ran hotly through her veins because she could feel him even now hard and ready through the fine layers of fabric separating them. Cheeks warm, she sat down, her knees no longer willing to hold her upright. Desire was spreading pulses of mortifying need through her entire body. She might get mad at him, he might often annoy her with what he said and what he did not say, but she never ever stopped wanting him back. Even though they still had a lot of undercurrents to steer safely across, she was determined not to think about them on their wedding day.

Polished, professional entertainment had been organised for the reception. Once they had eaten, Jace guided her round, ensuring that they spoke to all the guests and spending time with her father and half-brothers in particular. She could see that he found it a strain to exchange pleasantries with his own relatives, who had ignored him virtually until the very day of his father's death. She stepped in for him whenever she could, forcing herself to be a brighter, funnier and more outgoing person than she actually was, and it embarrassed her to appreciate just how much she wanted to protect him. Even when he was older, more sophisticated and a million times richer than she was? Yes, she acknowledged, even then. Where Jace was concerned there was a soft spot inside her that she couldn't harden.

Jace watched his cousins gather round Gigi on the dance floor, espied the spite glinting in Seraphina's hard eyes and narrowing them as she moved in Gigi's direction. He strode into the crush to steal his bride back to himself. He was damned if he would stand back and allow Gigi to suffer for one of his mistakes.

'Keep your distance from Seraphina,' he warned her soft and low as he steered her away from that group.

'I've already learned that lesson,' she admitted ruefully. 'She's a viper. What on earth did you do to her?'

'I'll tell you, only not here and now. But I will not tolerate her anywhere near us if she makes the mistake of targeting my wife with her nonsense.'

Gigi's eyes brightened at that possessive designation. 'I can look after myself, Jace.'

'But you shouldn't have to,' he responded in a tone of finality, his clean jaw line hardening with resolve. 'Particularly not when in any of the homes that we now share.'

'Gosh, you're being very inclusive all of a sudden,' Gigi murmured with a helpless giggle at the prospect of being included in the ownership of more than one home. 'How many properties do you own?'

'Six that I actually use, mostly inherited like the London apartment. My father hated hotels.'

Her fingers laced into the springy dark luxuriance of

his hair, dallied there and spread to the base of his skull to draw him down to her.

'No,' Jace told her succinctly. 'If you touch me, I'll do something indecent in public, so play safe and *don't* touch me.'

Pink and roused more than she liked by the hard slide of his body against hers, Gigi broke his embrace to step back from him. As she crossed the floor to speak to Electra, where she sat with her closest friends in a quieter corner, Evander Diamandis came to a halt in front of her and kissed her on both cheeks with enthusiasm. Gripping both her hands, he smiled down at her. 'Thank you for making Jace happy—'

'No,' she demurred. 'Let me thank you, your mother and Marcus for making me so very welcome.'

She had barely exchanged more than a few words with Jace's grandmother before Jace was ushering her away again and urging her to change for their flight. 'We're leaving *now*?' she carolled in surprise.

'We're spending our wedding night in Oman.'

Jace practically lifted her out of the SUV at the end of the long, potholed track.

The ultra-modern villa was well lit. He walked her into a sleek entrance hall that opened into an even more elegant and contemporary living space. An ice bucket complete with champagne and two goblets awaited them. Jace strode through to the kitchen and dug into the fridge to produce orange juice for Gigi.

'You've been here before,' she guessed as she sipped the refreshing drink.

'Several times when I was a teenager and adventuring was still in my blood. While Evander and Marcus played golf, I went off exploring.' As she set her empty glass down, he swooped on her to scoop her up into his arms. 'Right now, all I want is to explore you—'

'Just when I was about to ask you about Seraphina—'

Jace groaned out loud as he carried her up a flight of shallow steps and into a cool spacious bedroom decorated in warm creams spiced with subtle hints of jazzy orange and turquoise. 'It's a sad little story of immaturity. I was eighteen and drunk. She was twenty-two. I spent the night with her. The following day her father visited Evander and Marcus. He accused me of taking advantage of her and demanded that I marry her—'

'What?' Gigi exclaimed in surprise. 'You were only a teenager and she was older than you were!'

'It was completely casual but I did make the mistake of crossing those boundaries. It was a set-up, of course. I was supposed to marry her to protect her reputation but, to be frank, she was no more an innocent than I was.'

'Oh, dear…she told me that you were hers *first*.'

'No, I was fifteen the first time I dallied with a lady.' Jace rolled his eyes in acknowledgement. 'And you're my one and only relationship.'

'And I got pregnant,' she sighed as she kicked off her shoes.

'No, *we* got pregnant,' Jace countered, dropping down

beside her on his knees and pulling her into his arms. 'It does take two, you know…'

His warm mouth came down on hers with the kind of hunger that sizzled through her every nerve ending. Lean hands extracted her from her vest top and skimmed off her cropped linen trousers at speed, her lingerie vanishing at a similar pace. With an identical sense of freedom, she stripped off his shirt, stretching up to smooth reverent hands up over his muscular hair-roughened torso before he vaulted off the bed to peel off his chinos and his boxers.

He returned to her, a vision of bronzed masculine perfection and potent arousal, and kissed her breathless, clever fingers toying with the achingly sensitive peaks of her swollen breasts. 'Two weeks is too long for us to be apart—'

'It wasn't my choice,' she reminded him, slender fingers tracing the velvet smooth thrust of his erection.

'I thought it was best to let the dust settle—' But Jace gritted his teeth, knowing that he'd been craven when he had refused to admit that the baby announcement had knocked him for six, only he still did not feel up to the challenge of admitting that. Particularly not if Gigi might assume that he, who had once been rejected by his parents, was in some way now rejecting their child, because that was untrue.

'Never let the sun go down on a row,' she retorted in disagreement, silky, streaky strands of hair brushing his thighs as she bent her head to tease him with her mouth.

'I believed I was making the wisest move—'

'Well, when would you ever tell me or yourself that you'd been stupid?' Gigi jibed as his hips arched up to her and an almost soundless groan was dredged from him.

'Can't take that amount of torment, not right now,' Jace growled, suddenly hauling her up to him and rolling over to settle between her spread thighs. As she closed her legs round him in instant welcome, he tilted her back and surged against her tender cleft, discovering the warm wet heat of her and sending a current of electrifying anticipation through her quivering length.

'Exquisite…' He pushed inside her with a hushed groan of appreciation and angled his lean hips. Pleasure shimmied through her in heady waves as he stretched her inner walls with delicious force and friction. She flung her head back, her heart rate escalating as he began to move. The excitement began to climb, perspiration dampening her skin as she gripped him. A blinding wave of hunger powered her as he hammered into her at speed and the wild soaring excitement took over for endless moments. The intensity he induced sent her into an explosive, gasping climax that wrung her out.

'Sublime,' Jace pronounced, holding her close, his heart still racing against hers in the languorous aftermath. 'But for the record, I don't make stupid decisions—'

'Talk about it in the morning,' she whispered in cowardice, burying her hot face in the hollow of his shoulder and heaving an exhausted sigh.

'I was about to suggest a shower—'

'You get frisky in showers…wake me up at dawn,' she mumbled, feeling inexplicably secure and happy again.

In the morning, she wakened alone, however, which left her free to wash and dry her hair and slip into a blue and white sundress in honour of the scorching sunlight arrowing through the windows. Barefoot, she padded out to the outdoor terrace she had noted in the moonlight the night before and only then registered that it led out onto a clifftop platform suspended over the sea and the beach far below. There, Jace awaited her, a colourful breakfast already laid out in readiness for her.

'Wow,' she breathed in respect of that spectacular view of the Indian ocean, sunlight glimmering over turquoise seas that washed the edge of the long white beach.

'This is why the parents bought this place, plus Evander likes to golf and Marcus likes to sunbathe. I, however, simply want to spend time with you,' Jace murmured, closing a hand over hers as she dropped down beside him on the comfortable upholstered built-in seating.

'Where are the staff?'

'Maryam comes in at mealtimes only, unless we request otherwise—'

'And your security team?'

'In the housing at the foot of the lane. You should eat. We're leaving soon.'

Gigi poured her tea, sipped it, savouring the refreshment, grateful that the occasional bouts of nausea she suffered were still controllable as long as she ate little and often. 'Are we going to talk about stuff?' she asked stiffly, mentally bracing herself for that challenge.

'No. We're going to settle into being married first… and your objective is to learn how to relax and *rely* on me. You've lived through two frantic weeks of wedding excitement and naturally you're tired. Let me do the worrying for once,' he urged lazily, his thumb stroking the sensitive inside of her wrist.

Gigi breathed in deep. She did not rely on a man, never had, never would. She liked everything deep and hidden unearthed and out on the surface for her perusal. She wanted to know exactly how Jace felt about being married to her and a prospective father. But, being Jace, he had cut her off at the knees before she even gave her opinion. And what he wanted was crystal clear. There was to be no talking, no honest exchange of feelings and views or, indeed, any discussion about where their convenient marriage was even expected to go.

Her teeth gritted together. She cast him a glance that involuntarily lingered. In a white linen shirt, emerald eyes glittering, blue-black hair catching the sunlight, his lean dark classic features were breathtakingly handsome. Add in all the rest of him, the perfect physique, the little devil of teasing amusement that often danced in those eyes and the undeniable charisma he emanated, and he was a major challenge.

He was telling her to act like one half of a couple and she didn't know how to do that, didn't know how she was supposed to give him her trust when she already loved him. After all, give him trust as well and he would *own* her, hurt her with his indifference, his rich-boy polished wit and tantalising bedroom expertise.

'I'd just like to talk to you…in private,' Gigi told Achilleus Georgiou almost a month later.

'On the yacht?' Achilleus asked. 'Why not come to the restaurant and we'll sit in the courtyard and chat?'

'The yacht will be more private. Tomorrow? Around eleven? It's my day off.' Cramming her phone back into the pocket of her lab coat, Gigi made that decision for the older man and heaved a sigh. It was time to return her father's letters to him and hopefully that would finally open a line of communication between them and encourage her father to be honest.

It was the end of her second week back to work. Oman had been an amazing experience. They had travelled into the dramatic Jebel Akhdar mountains, dined on the edge of a magnificent canyon with the rugged mountains all around them, toured ancient tombs and forts and wandered through a deserted ghost village. Understanding her fascination and the reality that she had not travelled anything like as widely as he had done, Jace had promised to bring her back in the spring when

the damask roses would be in bloom and the air would
be full of their perfume. She had laughed and reminded
him that she would be too close to having their child to
fly anywhere.

There had also been lazy days on the beach with
intimate dinners on the terrace. They had explored
the walled old city of Muscat, sampled spices in the
souqs and admired the sunlit ambience of the low white
buildings with their ornamental Portuguese-influenced
balconies. For the first time in her life that she could re-
member, she had totally relaxed, allowing Jace to take
care of everything. And, given that freedom to manoeu-
vre and plan and organise, Jace had been in his element.

Their dinner had been served one evening by a camp-
fire in the Wahiba Sands and it had been a magical experience. She had even tried to sleep under the stars
before grumpily surrendering to her aches and pains and
clambering back into the top-of-the-line air-conditioned
RV Jace had hired for the occasion. He had laughed but
she had still enjoyed the splendid tawny sunset that had
rewarded their stay over breakfast. Jace had ruled out a
camel ride or even a trip in an SUV through the dunes as
too great a hazard for her in her pregnant state. His endless caution on her behalf had annoyed her once or twice
because throughout their honeymoon he had treated
her as though she were a fragile piece of china liable to
break if allowed to overtax herself. Fortunately for her,
he had not carried that approach into the bedroom with
her. It was mortifying too that she had allowed Jace to

ignore the issues between them but thinking about them only upset her.

A dreamy smile and a flush on her cheeks as she recalled that powerful passion of his, Gigi took her time tidying up her paperwork while Ioanna cast her knowing looks.

'What?' she finally paused to ask the nurse.

'You are just so in love with your husband…it's touching,' she opined with an apologetic smile. 'I don't know how you bring yourself to leave him every day.'

'Because he's working too,' Gigi pointed out wryly.

And had she got in the way of *his* work, he'd have driven her up the wall with his limitless energy. Round the clock, she had decided, Jace was best kept busy and occupied. If only she had that luxury, she reflected ruefully. No, she reminded herself dully, from now on, thanks to her pregnant state, she would only be working part-time hours. The arrangements were already in place.

Her new obstetrician in Rhodes town, a grounded, sensible woman, had warned her the week before that her blood pressure was dangerously high. She was to have less work and stress, more rest and daily walking and swimming exercise to try and bring the reading down to a safer level and lower the risks for her child and herself. All of a sudden, Gigi's pregnancy was dominating her life.

Only that morning, Jace had accompanied her to her most recent medical appointment, and she had had an ultrasound that had revealed the gender of their child. She was having a little girl. The joy of that discovery had been laced with anxiety for Gigi because now she knew that she could not have blind confidence in her own health. Jace had been delighted.

'She'll take some looking after,' he had remarked thoughtfully. 'She'll be the first heiress in the Diamandis family for several generations.'

Jace had made not one single comment when she was advised that only part-time work was viable for her until her blood pressure reduced. And if that didn't work, even more far-reaching changes of lifestyle would be required from her. Her soft mouth compressed and downcurved.

The dogs greeted her the instant she stepped off the launch because they sat down there awaiting her return every afternoon. Jace stepped out of the lift as she was halfway up the first flight of stairs. 'Lift…' he stressed gently. 'You're supposed to be taking it easy and four flights of stairs isn't easy.'

With bad grace and feeling rather like a dog who had pulled rudely on her leash only to be yanked back into line, Gigi retreated back down the stairs and joined him in the lift. As always, he looked amazing, black curls tousled by the breeze, compelling green eyes lighting up his lean, bronzed face, raw energy still emanating from him even after hours of business calls and meetings. And Gigi? She felt utterly drained, her hair descending untidily round her cheeks from her once elegant updo, her face bare of make-up, mud on her jeans from an over-enthusiastic cocker spaniel.

'Time for a drink,' Jace announced, shepherding her into the main saloon, where she flopped down like a legless puppet into a comfortable armchair. 'You're exhausted.'

'Was that a criticism?' Gigi hated the sharp edge that had entered her voice.

'An observation.' Jace slotted a moisture-beaded juice drink into her hand and settled a couple of glossy brochures down on the occasional table beside her.

'What are these?'

'Houses for sale on Rhodes. There's another one available but it's not officially on the market yet,' he volunteered. 'We need a home base other than the yacht.'

In silence, Gigi leafed through the small selection of very large, luxury homes on offer. 'We're perfectly comfortable here—'

'*Sea King* isn't a long-term solution. Not for us or the animals. And I assume you want to remain close to your father and brothers and the shelter, of course. We can continue to spend weekends on Faros but it wouldn't be feasible to live there. It's too far to commute—'

Gigi breathed in deep. 'Is it worth going to the hassle of buying and furnishing a house on a permanent basis?' she heard herself ask and, indeed, the question almost leapt off her tongue and it sounded a little tart. 'I mean…how long will our marriage last?'

The instant she said it, she regretted it and a chill ran

down her spine. Jace stilled and studied her in apparent astonishment. 'I haven't got a crystal ball but—'

'I'm sure that you could give me an estimate.' Gigi was wondering what devil had got into her or if her outspoken tongue was simply a horrible eruption of the insecurities she struggled with on a daily basis. After all, Jace had refused to address her right to know how he felt about her and their child. She had been fretting about that since before their wedding. It was time he answered some of her questions.

Jace's lean, hard-boned features were pale and taut. He expelled his breath in a stark hiss. 'I've always hoped that you would at least stay with me until after our child is born but—'

Gigi rose immediately upright, marvelling that she could stand when she felt as though he had plunged a knife into her chest. 'Perfect, we don't need to be looking at houses, then!'

'Even if we *were* to separate, Gigi, you and our child will need a proper home to live in on the island,' Jace asserted flatly.

Squashed flat by the lowering awareness that he had already calculated the practicalities of them separating, Gigi walked out of the room without looking at him again. Of course, of course, why hadn't she guessed what Jace intended all along? A marriage to legitimise their child and see it born and then soon after they would part, still being civil and friendly to co-parent. All of a sudden everything made so much more sense.

This had been his plan all along. This was why he had been willing to sacrifice his freedom, why he had been so impossibly delightful and soothing from the outset. Jace had always seen his escape on a not too far distant horizon. Anyone could contrive to make the best of a situation if it was only going to last for the duration of a single pregnancy. And, naturally, he hadn't wanted to make a point of saying that at the same time as he persuaded her to marry him. She suspected that he hadn't wanted his family to know that truth either.

Left alone, Jace downed two whiskies in record time. He had closed her out to keep his own emotions under control. He had withdrawn and she had noticed that he wasn't fully present or honest with her any more. Of course she had. How could he ever admit that he was terrified of losing her? Since the day she had married him, she had always had one foot out of the door.

And that was why he should not have mentioned the houses. Not when he knew that she was still agonising over having to accept working only part-time. Yet it was only for a few months. And how was he to straighten her out when she was supposed to be staying calm and resting as much as possible? He wasn't a miracle worker. Gigi seethed with emotion under her tranquil, collected surface but she didn't share her innermost worries with him... or trust him...or rely on him. So, what else wasn't new?

CHAPTER TEN

ACHILLEUS GEORGIOU SIPPED his coffee and studied his daughter with a frown. Her eyes were red-rimmed, her lovely face pale and strained, shadows suggesting a sleepless night. 'Tell me what's wrong,' he urged her, thoroughly disconcerting her with that personal question.

'There's nothing wrong,' Gigi hedged, even though she had barely slept the night before for fretting about losing Jace, losing her baby, losing Mo, losing *any* prospect of happiness. She had also fretted about her high blood pressure because now she had to doubt the healthy body she had once naively taken for granted. And then Jace, who had not come to bed with her because she had chosen to sleep with the dogs and the cat in the room next door, had greeted her at breakfast as though he had not a single care in the world. Furthermore, after learning that she was meeting with her father that morning, he had suggested that they lunch out later because she wasn't working. As if she were capable of enjoying a lunch out in the mood she was in!

'No, this is about something else,' she warned her father, lifting the bundle of letters from the bag she had stowed them in and extending them to the older man. 'I found them when I was cleaning out Mum's attic.'

Achilleus had stiffened and he went through the un-opened letters that spanned half a dozen years with frowning concentration. 'Did Nadine not even open them to read?' he muttered in dismay and astonishment.

'Apparently not…it's left me with questions I'd really like you to answer. What happened between you that she wouldn't even read your letters?'

'She said she would never forgive me if I left her and she kept her promise,' he acknowledged heavily. 'I need to start at the beginning. Katerina and I married as soon as we left school. We had the four boys, one after another, while I was building our first business. We hardly saw each other and ten years down the road she told me that she wanted a separation. I was devastated. At first, I didn't think she was serious. I moved in with my mother to give her some space to think but it didn't change anything. She went back to work and decided that she would be happier without me.'

Gigi had flushed with mortification because she had always doubted her mother's contention that her father had been separated from his wife when they met but now it seemed that that was true. Furthermore, it was disconcerting to learn that her father's marriage had broken down when they were both still young.

'Katerina and I lived apart for months and during that

period I met Nadine. Your mother and I fell in love and planned to make a life with each other—'

'How long were you and my mother seeing each other for?' Gigi cut in. 'I always assumed you'd only spent a few days together.'

'No. After our first meeting, we met up several times in London and Athens before Nadine realised that she had conceived. We were together about six months before that happened. I planned to get a divorce and move to London to set up a business there…but I'm afraid that turned out to be very much a fantasy.' Achilleus winced in embarrassment at that memory. 'But I was thrilled when Nadine told me she had conceived because I've always loved children. And then, unfortunately for all of us, real life and misfortune stepped in and what I had with your mother fell apart.'

'What happened?'

His face shadowed. 'First, I did my sums. I didn't have enough money to provide for Katerina and the boys *and* start a new life in London. Your mother wanted to pay for everything but I refused to live off her and she couldn't accept that. We began to argue—'

'She could only see her own point of view—'

'And she couldn't compromise about anything. She wasn't prepared to even consider moving jobs even after she was offered lucrative work in Athens,' he confided heavily. 'And then everything else went wrong all at once. Katerina got breast cancer. She didn't tell me… my mother told me. I couldn't leave Katerina alone to deal with the boys while she was undergoing chemo-therapy. There were problems with me trying to manage the business long distance as well. I came home because I *had* to. Understandably your mother was furious. She felt betrayed. We were a couple and I was leaving her to come back here to support my estranged wife—'

Gigi frowned. 'But your kids were still your respon-sibility.'

'But so were *you*—although at that stage you hadn't even been born. Nadine swore that if I returned to Rhodes, I would never be allowed contact with you. And that's basically the whole story. Your mother ig-nored my letters and returned any child support money I sent. But I still can't believe that she didn't even read my stupid letters!'

'I'm sorry it ended like that. I'm sorry that you tried to have a relationship with me but she wouldn't allow it—'

'I could've visited, not often but enough that you would have known me as your father!' Achilleus ar-gued plaintively.

Gigi leant forward and grasped his hand to squeeze it with sympathy because he had ditched his pride to tell her the whole story. 'It means so much to me that you *tried* to have a relationship with me,' she confessed. 'Why didn't you tell me all this when I first arrived on Rhodes?'

'It was so messy, and nothing can change the fact that I *did* let your mother down and she was entitled to be

bitter and unforgiving,' he said heavily, guilt hanging
over him like a dark cloud.

'You owed your first loyalty to the children you already had, and you had to support them as well. Mum
didn't neglect me. She wasn't the most affectionate of
mothers, but she did the job,' Gigi contended.

Tears shimmered in the older man's eyes and he
looked hurriedly away before vaulting upright and taking an uncoordinated walk round the room. 'I would
have loved you very much if she'd given me the opportunity.'

'I believe that.' And Gigi did. 'I gather that you and
Katerina found your way back to each other.'

'Yes. Her illness made us both grow up fast and we
grew together. It was hard for her to accept you when
you arrived on the island. She assumed that you would
hate her because I'd reconciled with her and that made
her feel uncomfortable.'

Gigi forced a smile. 'She needn't worry. My mother's
past isn't my present.'

But as her father was leaving, she did question her
own final statement. In truth her mother's past and
conditioning had always influenced her life. Nadine's
bitterness and distrust of men had given Gigi toxic expectations of the opposite sex and had made her afraid of
ever trusting a man or depending on one. Involuntarily,
she had brought that baggage into her relationship with
Jace, judging him before he even spoke, always making
assumptions, never giving him the benefit of the doubt,

invariably assuming the worst. She was in a troubled
mood of reflection when she joined him for lunch.

'Where are we going?' she asked.

'It's a surprise.'

'Do you think I'm in the right mood for a surprise?'
she muttered tightly.

'No, but you *need* one to lighten up…and we need to
talk,' Jace decreed, steadying her to step into the launch
with the dogs.

Her heart sank. What she had forced him into admitting the night before had made it impossible for them to
continue breezing along as though they were any other
newly married couple. Putting an end date on a marriage made a nonsense of that marriage being a normal
one. She had brought her mother's bone-deep pessimism
into her relationship with Jace and he fully recognised
the fact. It shamed her to accept that she hadn't had the
maturity to think for herself, hadn't once questioned her
low expectations of him or compared his actual behaviour to her damaging convictions.

The limousine pulled off the coastal road into a leafy
lane. Laced branches created a tunnel effect above them.
'Where on earth are we?' Gigi demanded.

'Wait and see,' Jace urged as the car pulled up outside
a big sprawling cream house and he sprang out, letting
the dogs run free as well.

'Have we met the owners?'

'They're not here. They've already moved to Corfu
to be near their daughter.'

'So, what are we doing here?'

'We're having a picnic lunch,' Jace told her cheerfully. 'Indoors. It's not really warm enough to eat outside.'

Withdrawing a key from his pocket, he herded her to the front door.

'I've never had an indoor picnic,' she confided.

'You haven't lived,' Jace teased.

But she could see that he was nervous. Probably about the necessity of them talking and exchanging damaging bouts of honesty. Such as he fancied the socks off her, couldn't keep his hands off her but didn't want to be married to her for ever. Fair enough. No, it wasn't fair enough, another voice said inside her. It was blasted unfair, after he had tempted her into falling in love with him.

Jace led her into a cosy entrance hall and she shivered even though she was only cold on the inside, cold with fear about what confessions they were about to exchange. 'So, talk,' she urged him with helpless impatience, not wanting to wait for the axe to fall.

Jace held up a silencing hand. 'We eat first.'

He thrust open a door into a spacious room packed with comfy seating. A tiled Scandinavian stove emanated heat in one corner. The windows overlooked more trees that parted to frame a view of the sea. An elaborate picnic basket awaited them on the table and he opened it to set out plates and food and drinks.

Self-conscious as always, her mind in turmoil, Gigi

ate several tiny snacks, prepared by their chef, and then embarked on a quiche. A sandwich in one hand, she paced the floor. 'That's a fabulous view,' she remarked.

'Do you want to tour the rest of the house?'

'We might as well,' she conceded as he drained his coffee cup and set it down to vault upright.

'Is this the house that isn't officially on the market yet?' she asked.

'Yes. It belongs to friends of Yaya's. If we like it, we can move in whenever we like and spend the winter here before we make a decision,' Jace told her.

Gigi strolled round, noting the spacious reception areas, seeing where updating would be required in utility areas. There was an indoor pool and a gym in the basement. She slowly climbed the stairs to find that there were plenty of bedrooms and a fabulous roof terrace, which overlooked the beach and the water.

'The house comes with several acres and it's very private—'

'It's a little big for one couple and a baby,' she remarked awkwardly.

Jace shrugged, striving to play it cool. 'But there might be more than one baby and then we'd be glad of the space,' he dared.

'I beg your pardon?' Gigi almost whispered. 'I thought you only wanted to stay with me until our daughter was born.'

'No, that is what I assumed you might decide when we first married but it was never *my* plan. I want to keep you until we're both old and grey, so room for more children in a house seems only sensible,' Jace countered steadily.

Gigi blinked rapidly, convinced she had imagined that statement.

'Of course, you're now about to come up with forty reasons why what I just said can't be true. But listen to *me* instead,' Jace suggested, hands closing over her arms to direct her to a seat in the corner of a big bedroom and gently push her down on it. He squatted down in front of her and gripped her hands in his. 'I'm sorry I checked out emotionally when we found out about the baby. I *was* in shock, but I wasn't willing to share that with you. I thought it would make you feel worse, so I attempted to focus on only the practical things, only that seems to have rebounded on me. I could feel that I was losing you…'

Suddenly she had the guy she loved back and he was finally talking to her again about what really mattered. She stroked the back of his hands with loving fingers.

Jace breathed in deep. 'I fell for you almost the same moment I met you, although it took me weeks to realise it. I don't know why I fell for you, so there's no point asking me why. Obviously, I was strongly attracted to you, but I love your personality even more. Your loyalty, your intelligence, your fondness for animals, your kindness, your warmth. I'm insanely in love with you and I can't face my life without you in it. Before you, it was empty, directionless, boring—'

'Jace…?' she whispered shakily, looking dizzily at him. 'Are you really saying this stuff?'

'Are you finally listening?'

'Of course I'm listening.'

'Getting you to the church felt like trying to catch a tiger by the tail and stick it in a cage. I wasn't at all sure I could persuade you to stay with me, but I'd have said anything to get that wedding ring on your finger. I mentioned the inheritance issue because it was practical, and you are always *very* practical. I didn't want to risk upsetting you by telling you that I felt more for you than you did for me. I didn't want you telling me that I was deluded or crazy to develop such strong feelings for you so quickly. So, I kept quiet because I was afraid of frightening you off—'

'I'm not going anywhere…you couldn't frighten me off,' Gigi told him dreamily. 'I'm mad about you as well and that has been such a worry because I had no idea at all you felt the same way. I just assumed you were being charming and nice because I was pregnant—'

Gorgeous green eyes collided with hers. 'You love me? Then why did you make me freak out last night by asking me how long you can expect this marriage to last? That was horrible!' he exclaimed with a look of strong reproof. 'I want you with me for ever and ever and you don't get time off for good behaviour or time to think about how you feel about me…you're *stuck* with me! I need to be with you—'

'I think I would quite like being stuck with you for

eternity,' Gigi admitted with a growing smile of happiness and the first sense of real relaxation she had experienced in months. It was a relaxation of tension, of constant worry and insecurity. The prospect of a real future with Jace filled her with pure, unalloyed joy.

Jace tugged her upright into the circle of his strong arms. 'Eternity mightn't be long enough, *glykia mou*. I'm fully committed and passionate about our marriage. And yet you fuss endlessly about all the small stuff. Like taking time off work when you'll only be restricted for a few months. I'll live anywhere in the world that you want…all I want is you and our daughter and I want you to be happy with me. You make me happy. It's simple enough.'

Gigi gazed up at him in growing wonder. 'I'm sorry I got so caught up in my work that I didn't realise what I was doing to you. Sadly, there wasn't anything but work in my life until you came along…and that was a major change for me. It made me vulnerable because I wasn't used to feeling what you make me feel. I've been worrying so much. I couldn't sleep last night—'

'Do you think I slept? You even took my dog with you,' Jace pointed out in reproof.

Gigi reddened and wrapped both arms round his neck. 'Only because he knows I'll let him into bed and you won't.'

'No dogs in our bed. That's an unbreakable rule,' Jace decreed.

Gigi pouted. 'I was going to tell you how much I loved you until you said that,' she teased.

'Not falling for it,' Jace warned, claiming a passionate kiss from her readily parted lips, edging her towards the bed.

'We can't…this isn't our house!' she exclaimed in dismay.

'We're about to become tenants. No reason we can't check out the bed. I mean, you do like this place, don't you?'

'Space for the dogs and us and our baby, what do you think? I like having the sea right on the doorstep,' she confided abstractedly, gazing up at him in slight amazement. 'You love me this much that you're happy to go the domestic route and lose your freedom?'

'Ecstatic. You're everything I didn't know I needed and my day looks a lot brighter with you in it,' he confided, spreading her across the bed, inching off her sweater by covert inches while kissing her, lean hands smoothing down over her slight frame possessively.

'Why did you tell your family I was pregnant before the wedding?' she queried.

'I was happy about it and I couldn't share that with you because you were freaking out. I was surprised by my own reaction. I realised that I was the guy who *wanted* to trap you with his child and it embarrassed me,' Jace admitted, gently tugging her out of her skirt. 'I don't think I could have hung onto you if I hadn't got you pregnant. I didn't think you were that struck with me. You were too suspicious of me. I wanted more from you from the start and I told myself all sorts of things before I realised that I loved you…and then it all seemed so simple.'

He made slow, careful love to her, gazing down at her with tender green eyes, and her heart felt as though it were swelling inside her chest. Happiness filled her to overflowing in the aftermath when he told her again how much he loved her.

'I fell for you the first night we had dinner…gosh, I was such a pushover!' she groaned in mortification.

'You were a total party pooper who went home and left me lying awake half the night fantasising about you,' he contradicted.

Gigi brightened and laughed. 'Serves you right. Oh, I have to tell you about my father…'

Jace listened, frowning several times. 'Your mother was hard on him. As I see it, he didn't have much choice.'

He talked about future plans for the house, one hand possessively splayed across the slight swell of her stomach.

Gigi snuggled close and listened. 'That unbreakable rule you mentioned about the dogs—'

'Not in the bed unless you want us to end up with a bed the size of Noah's Ark,' he quipped. 'You'll bring more dogs home in the future. You know you will. We'll make them comfy somewhere outside our bedroom… OK?'

'A Noah's Ark filled with dogs kind of sounds cosy to me,' she admitted drowsily.

'But we will have children as well,' he reminded her gently. 'And they might want to share our bed too. Go to sleep, Gigi…'

EPILOGUE

Five years later

As SHE CAME downstairs, careful in her high heels, Gigi smoothed down her dress. It was red, silky and it clung to every curve. It was right up Jace's street while also being suitably festive.

It was Christmas Eve, but their children still had to wait a week for the seasonal bounty of gifts. In Greece, gifts were exchanged on the first of January, St Basil's Day. Lyra, their four-year-old, was already so pumped up on Christmas cheer that another week of waiting for Ayios Vassileios might send her shooting for the stars. In respect of Gigi's British heritage, one gift would be given to the children on Christmas Day.

Nikolaos, their two-year-old, was trying to scale the giant stuffed reindeer by the front door, his pyjamas at comical half-mast as he sidled past the table with the floral arrangement Electra had sent them.

'Nikolaos!' Gigi intervened before he could send the giant vase of flowers flying.

Lyra grabbed him, scolding him firmly.

'It's time for bed,' Gigi told her children.

Actually, getting them into bed was like trying to herd cats up the stairs and into their respective rooms. Lyra chattered up a storm while grabbing the bedtime story she wanted and sliding below her duvet. She had inherited Jace's black curls and Gigi's blue eyes, his height and big personality laced with her mother's intelligence. Gigi's blood pressure had steadily dropped down to normal during her daughter's pregnancy and Lyra had been a textbook delivery.

Evander and Marcus swore that Nikolaos was Jace reborn. He hurtled headfirst into everything. He was a fearless, lively bundle of restless energy, the child most likely to be found clinging with one hand to a cliff edge while still laughing. But the reverse side of that extrovert nature was a current of fierce affection. As his mother sank down on the side of his bed, her son wrapped both arms round her and squeezed hard before wriggling down under his duvet. A paw appeared on the other side of his bed and, seconds later, a little black and white head nosed out. It was Houdini.

The little terrier had come into the household shortly after Hoppy had passed away, so at least they had still had a pet when Mo followed Hoppy at the age of nine, which wasn't a bad age for a wolfhound to reach. After Mo had come Roxy, a gangly, clumsy wolfhound puppy, who was so laid-back she was horizontal most of the time. Gigi tucked her sleeping son in and carefully scooped up Houdini to take him out to the landing. Tilly,

strolling along towards them, pounced in front of the
terrier and hissed, prompting Houdini to make a break
for the stairs.

Humphrey and Snowy still lived on Faros and Humphrey even had a lady companion but Electra's fond
hopes of the pitter patter of little tortoise feet had yet to
be realised. Electra had had a minor stroke the previous
winter and they visited her on the island most weekends.
They had bought the house in which Jace had initially
told Gigi that he loved her and, after that first deliriously
happy winter there as a couple, they had updated where
necessary and the house had slowly but surely turned
into their much-loved home. Even with staff, it remained
a somewhat messy, chaotic household that often took in
rescue animals for a little while, particularly when the
shelter was oversubscribed. Evander would look pained
while he stayed over Christmas and he would earnestly
suggest new and better ways of doing things. And they
would listen politely and then go on much as before.
Marcus, however, could sit in the middle of a hurricane
without turning a hair.

Gigi still worked full-time at the shelter although she
also took long breaks to enable them to have holidays.
And they had ranged far and wide over the years, satis-
fying Gigi's desire to explore foreign climes, while also
embracing all the time they could to enjoy simply being
a couple. She saw her father most weeks and had since
attended two of her brothers' weddings, the christen-
ings of their children and their birthday parties. She was

now fully accepted as a member of the Georgiou family circle and enjoyed a comfortable relationship with her stepmother, Katerina.

Loving Jace had brought Gigi more happiness than she had ever dreamt might be hers. She had her career, her children, but most of all, she had Jace and, although she would never admit it to him, her world revolved around him. He loved her and she felt that love every day, even when he wasn't able to be with her. He would phone or he would leave a note somewhere for her to find or send a gift.

Now as she picked her way down the stairs and heard the front door open, her blue eyes brightened. Jace came through the front door and she surged across the hall to greet him. 'Happy Birthday!' she carolled happily. 'The kids are in bed…and dinner is ready.'

Jace held her back from him to better enjoy what she was wearing. 'Like the dress…and the shoes,' he confided. 'Very sexy.'

Roxy sloped up to his side in her languid way and bumped his knee with her head before sprawling down at their feet in an untidy heap to go back to sleep.

'That's as much physical effort as she's made all day,' Gigi told him ruefully.

Houdini bounced out of a doorway and hurled himself at Jace, driven by frantic terrier energy. Gigi tugged Jace past the Christmas tree festooned in lights towards the dining room for their meal.

Before she could take a seat, Jace pulled her to him

and said, 'I was expecting to walk into a party here. How the hell did you dissuade Evander and Marcus from throwing the usual party open house?'

Gigi winced. 'I didn't. You're still getting your big party tomorrow night on Faros…a whole family affair,' she told him guiltily. 'Tonight is just for us.'

'Terrific planning, *koukla mou*.' Jace ran a caressing hand across the pouting curve of her breasts and she quivered. 'Can we take a rain check on the food?'

'Er…'

'Of course we can,' Jace decided, bending down momentarily to sweep her up into his arms and head for the stairs. 'Am I allowed to ask what my present is?'

'Don't be impatient,' she told him with a secretive little smile as he settled her down on the big bed.

'You look so beautiful in that dress,' he said thickly, lean fingers tracing the pouting curve of her lips. 'You wore red just for me.'

'If you like to think so, Mr Diamandis.' But it was absolutely true. Red was a colour that she always thought wore her rather than the other way round. Red attracted attention and she never liked that much, unless it was Jace's attention.

He leant over her and crushed her parted lips beneath his, his tongue delving deep, and a little shiver of excitement gripped her. 'I love you,' he breathed huskily. 'I'm saying it now in case I forget to say it later.'

'You won't,' she told him confidently, lifting her arms to allow him to lift the dress over her head.

'And my present?' he teased.

'I'm pregnant, just like you requested three months ago,' she told him quietly. 'And that is the only present you're getting from me. Our third and final children will be born in the summer—'

'Child*ren*?' he queried.

Gigi looked smug. 'Always be careful what you ask for. We're having twins, two little boys to keep Nikolaos on his toes,' she told him.

With a huge grin, Jace wrapped both arms round her and hugged her tight. 'Who is the most wonderful woman in the world? Best birthday and Christmas present *ever*!'

'If I didn't love you so much, I wouldn't have agreed.' The bedroom door shook a little as a small foot kicked it and a wail sounded. 'Sounds like Nikolaos is looking for his father,' Gigi teased.

She lay back on the bed like a shameless woman in her red lace lingerie and slowly relaxed while Jace cuddled his son and talked him back into bed. He reappeared in the doorway and she smiled at him, totally relaxed. He was gorgeous and he still took her breath away and made her tingle in secret places when she looked at him. He loved children. He had learned to hug. He never failed to make her feel good about herself. As he returned to her, she heard the pitter patter of Houdini's little paws head for their son's room and the nice cosy bed he had in there. Yes, Jace still wouldn't have dogs in the bed but what he didn't know didn't hurt him.

Opening her arms to welcome Jace back, she was still smiling, a woman who had found love when nobody, least of all her, had expected to find it, with the male who had turned out to be the guy of her wildest dreams.

* * * * *

If you just couldn't put down
Greek's Shotgun Wedding,
then you're certain to love these other
emotional stories
by Lynne Graham!

The Baby the Desert King Must Claim
The Maid Married to the Billionaire
A Contract for His Penniless Cinderella
Two Secrets to Shock the Italian
Baby Worth Billions

Available now!

HARLEQUIN
Reader Service

Enjoyed your book?

Try the perfect subscription for Romance readers and get more great books like this delivered right to your door.

See why over 10+ million readers have tried Harlequin Reader Service.

Start with a Free Welcome Collection with free books and a gift—valued over $20.

Choose any series in print or ebook. See website for details and order today:

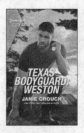

TryReaderService.com/subscriptions